HOW FAR
IS HEAVEN

J.E. SPINA

Table of Contents

HOW FAR IS HEAVEN

Published by J. E. Spina

Copyrighted by Janice E. Spina/J. E. Spina

DEDICATION

To my husband, John, who has been my rock, thank you for your patience and all the dinners you cooked so I could continue to write

To all my fellow authors who have been like a family to me and support me unselfishly, thank you

To my friend, Gloria, who asked me to write a novel with a little romance

ACKNOWLEDGEMENTS

Thank you to my beta readers, John Spina, Sally G. Cronin, Lorraine Price, Michele Rolfe, and Nortina Simmons, for their tireless efforts to read and review this book and for all their helpful input.

PROLOGUE

California - One hour after meeting

"Move the body now and take me back to my hotel room. I don't care what you do with him. Just make sure he disappears forever. You know who to call. He will know what to do."

"Okay, Boss. Is the pit okay?" The driver of the limo, Ned, looked up at his boss in the car's mirror waiting for an answer.

The boss just looked at him but didn't answer and added, "Did Buzz call back yet with the reports I requested?" The boss, a very distinguished older man in the back seat of the limo, asked his driver, irritation evident in his voice, while he completely ignored the question that his driver had just asked him.

"Um, well, no I haven't heard back from him. Do you want me to call him for ya, Boss?" Ned's voice audibly betrayed his fear of this man for whom he worked. He had seen Boss in action and knew what he was capable of. Boss had dismissed other drivers for minor infractions and they were never seen or heard from again. He knew he had to watch his back or he would end up like the others, gone forever.

"No, but I want to hear as soon as he does call. I gave him a job to do. Now take me to my hotel."

"Yes sir, Boss, right away," Ned was relieved that his boss' anger was directed elsewhere. He only hoped Buzz would call or the boss would become more ornery until he did.

As they arrived at the hotel the boss turned to Ned before getting out of the limo and instructed him in a stern voice, "The packages I gave you must be delivered to the drop off today. I want you to get them there as quickly as possible. Do you understand, Ned, or do I have to spell it out for you?"

"No sir, Boss. I'll do exactly as you say. I'll get the packages there for you by FedEx ok? I'll make sure they go out today. Is that ok? Boss?" Ned was never given his boss' name, just told to call him Boss. Ned never asked why because those who did…well, they just disappeared.

Ned was getting more nervous by the minute and just wanted to do these two jobs and then go home and drink himself to sleep as he usually did. Ned hoped that Buzz would hold up his end of this job and not screw up. If he didn't, it could be the death of both of them. Ned just couldn't understand why

Buzz hadn't called back by now. What was taking him so long?

He knew why Boss kept Buzz on the payroll, he was the boss' cousin's son. Boss knew Buzz was a loser but thought if he taught him the ropes he would come around to his way of thinking and doing things. Ned didn't think so. He had covered once before for Buzz but got no thanks from him for doing that. Ned decided to cut ties with him and let him hang himself this time.

***

Back in Maine Buzz was driving around Leah Mills to do his boss' bidding. He had been requested to check out the JemsWorld store and see what he could find out about its location and how profitable it was. The boss had designs on it and wanted to know square footage and accessibility to highways and airports.

Buzz walked through the store taking notes and asked to speak with the manager.

"Yes, sir I am one of the managers. How may I help you?"

"I am from the Department of Sanitation and want to see your warehouse." Buzz quickly flashed a badge he had made for the occasion and put it away before the man could take a closer look at it.

"Is there a problem?"

"Well, not yet, but after I take a look at it I will let you know." He smiled as the manager readily agreed to take him on a tour. Buzz could see the fear in this man's eyes and this fact only made Buzz feel more powerful and in control.

***

The movement of the vehicle woke him. He tried to sit up but found he couldn't move in the confining space. His hands and feet were fastened with plastic ties which rubbed painfully against his skin. He looked up and around him but it was too dark to see anything. His head throbbed and he felt as if he was going to be sick. He tried to clear his head to remember what had gotten him into this predicament. He suddenly remembered and said a silent prayer.

The vehicle came to a stop. He could hear footsteps coming closer then stopping at the back of the car. The trunk was opened and a large figure loomed over the man. The night sky was dark but the full moon was bright and the man had to blink in order to make out a tall, wide silhouette leaning over him. He tried to fight and was rewarded with a punch to the face knocking him out again. The man's last thoughts were of his family and his prayer for God to watch over them.

The body was heavy but the man was strong and he hefted the body over his shoulder and headed for the pit. All he had to do was throw the body into the pit but the boss told him to shoot first and then dump the body and cover with enough dirt until the cement was scheduled to be poured the next day.

CHAPTER ONE

Parker Wilfork

Parker smiled just thinking about his children and how excited they were about the surprises he always promised them when he returned from his business trips. Parker was still smiling as he exited the plane to meet the man who had emailed him to do business and had booked and paid for Parker's one-way flight to California.

Parker was so anxious to get back home that he had already booked a return flight home two days away. He had given his flight information to Priscilla the morning she drove him to the airport. She had promised to meet him at the airport in two days.

Yesterday Parker had second thoughts about going to California. He didn't even know this man who had paid for his flight. Parker had received an email from this man who had seen the flyers he had left in his travels to different states about setting up a JemsWorld store. All the man had told Parker was that this proposal he wanted to discuss with him would make him a rich man. The man had also told Parker to destroy the email after reading and not to discuss this with anyone. Parker liked the sound of this proposal making him a rich man since he did not want to be dependent upon his wealthy parents. What he didn't like was having to destroy the email. That didn't make any sense. What made him dismiss this was how Priscilla felt about asking his parents for any kind of help. She was very independent and could be extremely stubborn about such things. He was doing this for her and their children.

What Priscilla did not know was that Parker was doing extremely well in his business even though all his assets were tied up in the store. He had wanted to surprise her with added revenue especially if this new business proposal went through in California.

If everything worked out, Parker would move his family to California to open a new store in a super mall. This would mean big money. The idea of more money that was liquid would be welcome. Parker's flyer had stated he was looking for new places to open his stores. This man's proposal had intrigued Parker and he wanted to know more about it.

Priscilla's flawless skin and long blonde hair cascading around her angelic face suddenly came into Parker's mind. Parker felt his face redden as he thought of Priscilla's slim firm body under his as they had both reached a peak the night before. Parker had held Priscilla as he had run his fingers up and down her elegant and smooth back. An ominous feeling came over him as he felt Priscilla's body relax and her breathing become deeper. What if he was making a mistake by going to this meeting? He couldn't help feeling misgivings since the dream he had the night before. In this dream he was suffocating and couldn't move. He felt like was in a tight, dark place. He tried to look around but couldn't move his head because of pain and dizziness any movement caused. He had woken up in a sweat. At the same time he felt he needed to do this in order to provide independence and security for his family. He only hoped that he wasn't making a mistake.

Some people called them "Ken and Barbie" because of their good looks. Both of them had blond hair and blue eyes and were tall, slender and well fit. What people didn't see were the troubled childhoods both had had and how messed up they felt inside. Most people didn't look beyond their well-covered veneer.

Parker was a very lucky man to have Priscilla and their beautiful children even if he didn't have a lot of money right now, most of it being in his business and not readily liquidated. What was money after all?

Growing up he had seen how money had affected his parents. They were not very warm people especially to him and his siblings. His parents thought only of material things and how much more they could acquire. He did not want to become like his parents. He promised himself that if this business opportunity became reality he would use the money to do good for his family and others who needed it.

In order to distance himself from his parents Parker had started his own business from the bottom up with his own money. He had applied for some loans and brought in a couple of minor partners to help him purchase JemsWorld store, which was a derelict warehouse, and turned it into a beautiful department store. He had paid down some of the loans painstakingly by working around the clock. Parker had planned to own the business outright by the time he was thirty-five years old. That was only five years away.

His main objective was to be fair to the customers, treat them right and offer them competitive and affordable prices. Parker was rewarded with regular customers who brought in other customers by word of mouth. He was also known and respected by all his employees as a kind and generous employer. He gave his employees bonuses at Christmas time and rewarded all those employees who put in any extra time and care to help keep the customers happy. Business was very good and he was starting to realize a profit, the reason why Parker was contacted by this man. The man evidently saw promise in the JemsWorld store.

Parker shook his head to clear these thoughts. He had to keep his wits about him. His main concern now was this man and his proposal. Parker had to think about what to tell Priscilla about this last minute trip to California. He decided to tell her that it was a meeting about store business. I guess it was somewhat, he thought. He just didn't want to tell her about a possible move with his business.

When Priscilla wasn't too happy about him leaving, Parker promised to make plans to take the family on a trip to Disney World after he returned home from this business trip. It would be warmer in Florida than Maine in the fall.

Parker knew that Priscilla would not like the idea of moving from their little town of Leah Mills to live in California. He could not tell her about this new proposal until he was sure it would be profitable enough for them to move. He would somehow convince her that it was a good thing to do.

The man had told Parker that he would meet him at the Charter Bus Stop outside the airport and bring him to his hotel where they would discuss his proposal. The man said his driver would be holding a sign with his name on it.

As Parker exited the double automatic doors of the airport he looked up and saw a short, stocky but muscular man dressed in a dark suit holding a sign as instructed. The man was standing next to a large, sleek black limousine. Parker walked toward the man, identified himself and handed the man his luggage to put into the trunk of the limousine. This man who was the driver opened the door of the limo for Parker. As Parker entered the back seat he noticed another man sitting there who beckoned him to enter.

Once Parker was seated comfortably he looked with some anxiety at the stern face of the man dressed in an expensive-looking dark blue silk suit. The man then surprisingly smiled at Parker to put him at ease or maybe just to throw him off a little, Parker mused.

"Well, Mr. Wilfork, I presume you had a good flight? Would you like a drink? I have some fine scotch here," the man motioned to a bottle nearby.

Parker met the man's steady gaze but shifted in his seat, "My flight was fine. No thank you, I don't want a drink. Would you please tell me what this proposal is that you mentioned to me and who you are? I'm anxious to get this meeting over with so I can return home to my family," Parker uttered with some strain and anxiety evident in his voice. He was feeling anything but safe in this vehicle with this man. Parker was suddenly feeling that what this man would have to say to him would only cause him grief and trouble. Parker had noticed as he was bending down to get into the limo that the driver, holding the door for him, was wearing a gun. Parker had felt a lump in his throat and a sick feeling in the pit of his stomach. He should have backed away and not gotten into the limo when he had the chance.

The man eyed Parker and noticed his strained demeanor as he said, "Of course, Mr. Wilfork, my name is Byron. There is no need for a last name. I have a proposition for you. I am a contractor and a business man currently working on a very lucrative site here in California in Los Angeles. I am planning to put in a first of its kind super mall and want to set up a JemsWorld store as a base store in the mall. I have been watching your business grow. You are running a very profitable business and I want a piece of it. I have drawn up a contract and all I need is for you to sign right here on the line signing over the Maine store to me. I will move it to California once the mall is complete then I will close the Maine store."

Parker took the contract and started reading it. He frowned as he read the last paragraph. He handed the contract back to Byron and shook his head.

"I can't sign this contract. You are taking over all my operations back home in Maine. I cannot do that. I do not own the store outright yet. I have partners who would need to be consulted no matter what I do. What about my customers in Maine? I can't just close up shop on them. I was under the impression that you were building a mall and wanted a JemsWorld store and needed me to set it up and run it. If I did this I would not close the Maine store but keep it running for my customers with my partners taking on the role of managers. I own the name JemsWorld and this is my store."

Parker's head was spinning with this revelation. He realized he had made a terrible mistake. This man did not want Parker to move his operations to California and run his store there. He just wanted to take control of JemsWorld store and Parker's good reputation with it.

"Oh, now Mr. Wilfork, I know you control 51% of the business so that tells me that you have final say. Of course, you could tell your partners that you are going to do this and they would have to go along with you. I have a suitcase here full of money as an incentive, five million dollars to be exact. Just think about how much you could buy for your wife and children with this much money. You could take it and just walk away and find another company to start or not work at all. You could live comfortably without ever working again and just put some of your money into sound investments and watch it grow."

"Wait a minute, how do you know that I own 51% of the store?"

"Ha, I do my research, Mr. Wilfork. I know a lot about your store. Oh, I see what you are doing, Mr. Wilfork. You want more money, is that it? Five million is not enough? Well I can sweeten the deal and make it six million. All you have to do is sign right here now and we have a deal. I will even pay for your passage back home first class."

"I may be a fool to say this but, I don't understand why you are offering me so much money. My business is not worth that much. This just doesn't sound right to me. Just what are you trying to do? Why are you so interested in my store?"

Granted JemsWorld store was becoming a profitable store and becoming more so each year but not five million dollars' worth.

"Well, Mr. Wilfork, I have my reasons. You do not need to know what my business is with your store. All you have to do is sign on the dotted line and you can walk away with five or six million dollars and no cares and no worries. You can buy off your partners if you are feeling guilty about this sale."

"No, I will not sign this. Something is not right here."

Five million was more money than he would ever see in a lifetime but he had heard of men like this. Parker feared that this man knew what to do to businesses like his. He couldn't be part of this scheme. He ran a legal and family-oriented store and wanted to keep it that way. He may be crazy not to take this money and run but he had a conscience and could not live with the decision to be part of an illegal operation whatever it might be.

"Now I must be on my way to my hotel so I can get some rest before I head back home." Parker pulled the door handle of the limo and finding it locked angrily looked back at Byron who was now holding a gun to his head.

"Well, Mr. Wilfork, I didn't expect such an attitude from you. My sources told me that you would not give me any trouble. I guess they were wrong. You will just have to cooperate with me or you will not be going anywhere. Now, where were we? Oh yes, here is the contract and a pen. You know where to sign, don't you?" Byron handed the silver pen to Parker as he smiled in triumph knowing that he never had any intention of giving Parker the money or letting him leave. After all, he was a business man in the business to make money.

CHAPTER TWO

Priscilla Wilfork

Priscilla found her mind wandering as she drove through the little town of Leah Mills on her way to pick up her children. Leah Mills was a peaceful and lovely place to bring up children away from the hustle and bustle and dangers of the big cities. Priscilla had always been a country girl and very seldom did she venture out to the big cities of Bangor or Portland. She was content to stay in her little town, keeping busy caring for her children, volunteering at their school and doing her crafts. She loved to sew, crochet, paint and even dabbled in writing short stories and poems.

Priscilla loved Leah Mills and being away from and independent of Parker's parents. Well, Parker's parents were another story and from a different world, she thought.

***

Priscilla knew that Parker was more of a big city guy. He grew up in Kelton, Maine which was a lot bigger than Leah Mills.

Priscilla remembered the day she first met Parker's family. Parker had made plans to bring her to his parent's home for dinner as a way to introduce her to his family.

Priscilla was nervous but agreed to go but voiced her reticence, "Parker, I want to meet your parents but I don't know if I fit in to their way of life."

"Priscilla, I love you and want to marry you whether my parents accept you or not. It doesn't matter to me. Do you understand?"

"Yes, of course, Parker. I love you too but...."

"There are no buts here, my love. Let's just go have dinner and announce that we are going to be married. I am only doing this as a courtesy to them. You have to understand that I am not close to my family because of the way we were brought up. Well, you will understand when you meet them. Don't let them upset you, okay?"

Now Priscilla was really anxious after this announcement. What did his parents do to him as a child to make him feel so distant from them?

Parker drove up the long drive of his parent's home lined by beautiful maples and oaks and flowers of all varieties. The lawn was lush and green and had berms of decorative trees, statues and more flowers arranged to perfection by professionals.

Priscilla was awe struck by the opulence and beauty around her but the greens didn't prepare her for the enormous house that suddenly appeared ahead.

It looked more like a castle with porticos and a spacious, extravagant porch that ran from one end of the house to the other. On this lovely porch were cozy chairs and tables set up in inviting groups. Hanging plants were placed symmetrically between the porticos.

Priscilla loved the porch and the homey feeling she felt in spite of the large size of the house which was a Georgian Colonial three stories high with a tower in the middle.

She looked around trying to take it all in as Parker parked the car and opened her door. He extended his hand to Priscilla and helped her out of the car like the gentleman that he was.

Priscilla smiled and felt herself relaxing a little. The front door opened and out came Parker's parents walking stiff and straight with serious expressions on their stern faces. Gone was the relaxed feeling that Priscilla had fleetingly felt.

Parker squeezed Priscilla's hand and led her forward to meet his parents with the frozen faces. Parker extended his hand to his father and pecked his mother lightly on the cheek with no reciprocation on her part. His mother's eyes never left Priscilla's face as she waited for an introduction by her son.

Parker pulled Priscilla up to his parents as he began his introduction. "Mother, Father, this is Priscilla, my fiancé."

Priscilla extended her hand and it was taken by both parents in a light and feathery touch as their eyes appraised her. An audible gasp could be heard from both of them at the sound of the word, fiancé.

"Priscilla, this is my mother and father, Tran and Marion Wilfork."

"It is nice to meet you Mrs. & Mrs. Wilfork." Priscilla smiled as she appraised them back.

"Let's go inside, shall we?" Marion Wilfork turned and moved into the house exchanging raised eyebrows with her husband.

Waiting inside were Parker's three siblings, his sister, Susanna, and his twin brothers, Cole and Darien. They looked uncomfortable and awkward as they went through the same introductions and hand shaking with Priscilla. They looked anything but happy to be there.

Priscilla sighed and squeezed Parker's hand as they were led into the dining room where the extensive table was set up. The table was so long it could have seated twenty-four people at one time.

Maids and a butler were at the ready and the meal began in short order. No one spoke until the first course was laid in front of them.

Marion Wilfork began the conversation, "Well, Parker, what are you presently doing for work?"

"I bought a warehouse and will be converting it to a department store. I have two partners who have invested into it to help me out. Hopefully it will be up and running over the next several months."

"I see. A store you say? Hmm, well what do you think, Tran, about this?"

"If this is what he wants to do with his life, who am I to stop him? He is of age to do whatever he chooses, Marion."

"Of course, I know that Tran!"

Turning toward Priscilla, Marion asked, "What do you do for a living?"

"I am an artist. I also dabble in arts and crafts and writing."

"Do you think that you can make a living as an artist or dabbling in artsy stuff?" Marion stared at Priscilla.

Parker interjected to avoid any further comments from his mother. "Mother, Father and everyone, I would like to make an announcement. Priscilla and I are going to be married as soon as we can finalize the arrangements. You are all invited. I will send you the information of where and when."

"What? Are you kidding me? When did you meet?" Marion expressed her displeasure and surprise.

"We have known each other from college. I knew I wanted to marry Priscilla the first day I met her." Parker smiled at Priscilla showing how much he loved her.

Then the interrogation began. Priscilla was peppered with questions from Marion as she tried to answer one question before the next was asked.

Priscilla filled Marion in on her parents and the tough life in which she had to grow up. Marion voiced her opinions with a humph or two.

***

Life was hard for Priscilla and her brother, Merrill.

Their father had lost his job at the local feeds plant and numerous other jobs on several occasions. This forced their mother to go back to work days as a hairdresser in their home so she could watch over them and as a cashier in a drug store in the evenings and other jobs just to keep her children fed and clothed.

People used to whisper behind their backs about their dad always being out of work. Merrill didn't seem to be affected by this talk. It bothered Priscilla more though in the beginning but then she learned to ignore the talk and the ignorant people. She knew her father was a good man. He just wasn't a strong man in character or health. He liked to drink and most of the time he was sleeping off a drunken stupor.

Her mother told her that her father had suffered from back pain resulting from a fall many years ago on some ice in the parking lot at work as he was walking to his car. He had refused to go to the doctor right away until he couldn't stand the pain any longer. He had to be on pain medication for over a year just to relieve some of the excruciating pain. It seems that her father got addicted to the prescriptions and when he couldn't get them any longer he turned to booze. He evidently didn't put in a claim or complain about his injury until a few weeks after his fall and therefore was refused any compensation from the plant. He couldn't prove his accident had happened when and how it did.

Priscilla remembered her Dad before he started drinking though. He was wonderful to her brother and her, always playing with them. Each year he would give them a special surprise at Christmas time. It would be something that he would make himself. He was an excellent carpenter and could do wonders with a piece of wood. She still had the wooden angel and a dog that he had made for her when she was eight and nine years old respectively. She couldn't part with them for they were all she had left of her father. Her brother had a soldier and a tiger. She knew Merrill treasured his wooden toys as much as she did hers.

Their parents died when she was a teenager, seventeen to be exact. They had gone to a New Year's Eve party at one of their friends' houses across town. It had been a snowy night and the roads were slippery. Her father had had too much to drink and insisted on driving them home since her mother did not have a driver's license. Well, the combination of his drinking and the slippery roads were too much for her father. He lost control of the car on a patch of ice and plowed into a telephone pole which killed him instantly and severely injured her mother. Her mother died in the hospital later that same night.

Priscilla knew about death but did not know much about living. She prayed to God that night to save her mother but He didn't listen to her. She stopped going to church after that and even stopped praying.

***

Priscilla looked at Parker pleading for a respite as his mother's barrage of questions went on.

The end of the dinner couldn't come soon enough for Parker and Priscilla. They excused themselves and begged off dessert and coffee so they could make their escape with quick goodbyes.

Priscilla felt her heart pounding and her breathing difficult as she sat in the car waiting for Parker to start the engine and pull away.

Parker could see how upset Priscilla was and didn't speak for the first fifteen minutes. Thereafter he begin his tale of his childhood with cold and unfeeling parents.

"I am sorry for the way my parents treated you, Priscilla. I should have prepared you more. My parents are rich, filthy rich. They inherited oil money from both of their parents. My siblings and I were treated as property and never knew what it was like to have loving parents. They were always cold and distant with us growing up and I moved away from home as soon as I could, so did my siblings. My sister, Susanna, is living in Texas with her husband; and my twin brothers, Cole and Darien, moved to New York to pursue their dreams to go into show business. As you could see, my siblings were uncomfortable being in the house with our parents too."

"I don't know how you grew up so well adjusted and kind as you are, Parker. You, fortunately, did not inherit their cold traits. For that, I am grateful."

Parker caressed Priscilla's face tenderly in response. "I don't want to see you unhappy, Priscilla. Please don't let my parent's cold demeanor hurt you in any way. I don't expect them to come to the wedding. That is fine with me. I will be happier without them."

"Oh Parker, I don't want you to be without your family. I will have my brother and you should have your parents and siblings there too."

"It's all up to them. If they come, fine. If not, fine," Parker said with little emotion.

"Priscilla, let's not talk about this anymore. I want to concentrate on us and our life together from this day forward. Okay?" Parker smiled disarmingly at his love, attempting to end the tension and put the unpleasant evening behind them.

Priscilla smiled wanly and assented, "I agree Parker. I want to forget the evening altogether. I found it extremely uncomfortable and disconcerting. I feel sad about your parent's attitude toward our marriage. If that is how they feel then there isn't anything we can do to change their minds. All I know, Parker, is that I love you and want to be with you for the rest of my life."

"Ah, now you are talking some sense. I feel the same way, my love. I look forward to our life together. Let's put all our energies into making our life wonderful and less on my selfish and rude parents. It is their loss, my dear."

"Yes, honey. We will have a fantastic life." Priscilla said but not without some sadness for his parents.

Priscilla and Parker had their simple wedding ceremony with just a few friends from their past along with her brother, Merrill and his wife, Carolyn.

CHAPTER THREE

A Rough Time Ahead

Parker and Priscilla had been married almost seven years now. Their anniversary was next week, she thought, as she drove to the airport to pick Parker up after his business trip to California. Priscilla found a parking space close to the terminal and waited for Parker to come off the plane. He had given her an airline flight number the day he left and said he would call if there was a change. The children were all excited to see their father and anticipated the gifts he had promised to bring them.

They watched as several people get off the plane, the doors closed and the plane taxied to another hangar. When Priscilla didn't see Parker she took the children out of the car and brought them in with her. At this time the children were getting antsy as Deanna asked, "Where's Daddy?"

Priscilla tried to keep her patience in check as she answered, "We're going to find him, honey."

They proceeded to the baggage area to find Parker. He was nowhere in sight among the other passengers waiting there. She needed to speak to someone about her husband's flight and why he wasn't on it. She went up to an attendant for the airlines Parker had been on, Atlantic Airlines.

The attendant at the window told her that all the passengers had alighted and that there was no passenger by the name of Parker Wilfork on the flight list. Priscilla had tried at that time to remain calm and not let the children see the fright or shock in her eyes.

"Are you sure he is not on the passenger list?" Priscilla questioned the airline agent. "Could he have missed his flight and then booked another one later on? Could you please check other flights for me?" Priscilla responded in a trembling voice.

"I will check the other flights coming in today and tomorrow. One moment please, Ma'am." The attendant turned her attention back to her computer screen as her fingers tapped the keys in rapid order.

Priscilla held tightly to her children's hands as she swayed back and forth from one foot to the other. Her nerves were beginning to fray while she waited for an answer.

"I am sorry, Ma'am, but he is not on any flights today or tomorrow. But wait, I see him listed as a no show on today's flight. I did scan the flights all this week but he is not listed as rescheduled. I am sure he will call you and let you know what flight he will be on soon." The attendant responded to Priscilla clearly impatient to get back to work. But when the agent noticed the tears in Priscilla's eyes threatening to fall, she added, "You can call me back later tomorrow if you want me to recheck the new flights. I may have more information on future flights by then."

"No show?" Priscilla questioned clearly confused.

"Yes, Ma'am. If a person doesn't show up for their flight they are listed as a no show."

"I see. Okay, thank you." Priscilla mumbled as she steered her children out of the airport through the double doors. Priscilla found herself shaking but managed somehow to buckle up the children into their car seats and drive back home. Her mind was whirling and she couldn't think straight. She was in shock. She still couldn't believe that Parker had been not on the flight. *Why didn't he call me? Where was he? I haven't heard from him in two days .I called him that first night but he didn't answer. I should have tried again. I just thought he was probably sleeping and didn't want to disturb him. He had promised to call me as soon as he could. But why didn't he call?*

Deanna, at an inquisitive six years old, asked continuously on the drive home, "Where is Daddy?

How come he didn't come off the plane? When is he coming home?"

Robbie, at two years old, was still too young to realize anything was wrong. Priscilla tried to explain to Deanna, "Daddy must have taken a different flight. He will call us soon to let us know when to pick him up." Priscilla was hoping for the same thing but didn't understand why he hadn't already called her.

Priscilla pulled out her cell as soon as she arrived home and after ushering the children into the house she tried calling her husband's cell phone. She waited hopefully for Parker to answer but it just kept ringing and not going to voicemail. Next she looked up the phone number for the hotel Parker had booked, the Hotel Los Angeles. She waited impatiently tapping her nails on the side of the phone.

"Hotel Los Angeles. How may I help you?"

"Oh, yes, my name is Priscilla Wilfork and I would "like to be connected to my husband's room, Parker Wilfork, please."

"One moment please…I am sorry, Ma'am, there is no Parker Wilfork staying here."

"What, what did you say?"

"There is no Parker Wilfork staying here, Ma'am."

"This is the hotel he gave me. Please look again. You must be mistaken." Priscilla's voice shook as she tried to keep her nerves under control.

Priscilla felt her stomach turning over and feared she was going to be physically sick.

"No, Ma'am... this is correct. I do not have any Parker Wilfork listed. Is there anything else I can do for you?"

"No, maybe he gave me the wrong hotel. Thank you." Priscilla abruptly hung up the phone feeling more confused than ever.

Priscilla kept herself busy by cooking their favorite dinner for her children. They sat around the kitchen table and ate in silence except for the non-stop babbling of Robbie about his favorite TV shows.

Deanna ate and didn't look up at her mother until Priscilla spoke. "Deanna, honey. Are you feeling all right? You haven't eaten much of your mac and cheese."

"I'm not hungry, Mommy. Why didn't Daddy come home?" Tears were brimming in Deanna's eyes as she asked this.

"Honey, I don't know yet. Daddy will be calling us soon to tell us when he is coming home. Okay? Try to eat something, sweetheart. Then we can sit and watch a little TV and then I will give you both a bath." Priscilla smiled at Robbie as he shoveled in his favorite food. At least one of them was hungry tonight. She didn't have an appetite either.

Deanna grunted, "Okay, Mommy," and put a few pieces of macaroni into her mouth and chewed mechanically.

Priscilla was emotionally drained with worry about what could have happened to her husband. She tried not to let her children see the strain on her face.

She cleaned up the kitchen and got the children settled in front of the TV to watch a Disney movie. She grabbed a cup of coffee, placed it on the coffee table and sat down next to them wrapping her arms around them to comfort them and herself.

Priscilla thought back over the night before Parker left. She had held him in her arms and had an ominous feeling as if it was to be their last embrace. She couldn't put her finger on why she was feeling this way but it was a strong premonition. She had some of these feelings before her parents had died but refused to believe them.

Parker had been tender with their lovemaking as he had trailed kisses down her body. Their bodies had glistened after exertion as they trembled with release. Priscilla felt new tears forming and shook them off.

She had been lost in her thoughts and hadn't realized that the movie had ended until Deanna shook her and asked, "Mommy, I want to go to bed now."

"Oh, I'm sorry honey, I didn't realize that the movie was over. Let's get you both in the bathroom. Let me wash Robbie first then you can go next. Okay?"

"Can't I just go to bed, Mommy? I'm tired."

"I think you will feel much better after you bathe and are nice and clean. I will be quick with Robbie's bath. Now, go get your PJs and come back to the bathroom."

Deanna walked away with her head down to do what her mother asked. "Okay, Mommy."

Once the baths were over both children looked ready to go to sleep. She, too, felt worn out from all the stress and worry.

Priscilla looked at Robbie as he nestled close to her, "Night, night, mama." Priscilla held onto her precious little boy and whispered back, "Night, night, little man, sleep tight. I love you, sweetie pie." Priscilla flipped on the Spiderman night light before she closed Robbie's door and went next door to her daughter's room to check on her.

"Deanna, it's time to go to sleep now, sweetheart," Priscilla pulled up the covers and tucked them in around her daughter.

"Mama, did Daddy call yet? When is he coming home? I miss him. He promised that he would be bringing us a surprise from his trip." Deanna put down the book, *Lamby the Lonely Lamb,* she was pretending to read and looked up at her mother.

"I know, dear. He will call soon. Of course he will not forget to bring you a surprise. He always does, doesn't he?" Priscilla tried to keep her voice steady and upbeat. She wasn't sure when Parker would call or where he was.

Priscilla bent down and kissed her daughter's soft cheek and smoothed her hair away from her face. "Now it's time for you to get to sleep. I am sure we will hear from Daddy by tomorrow. Don't worry my sweet one. I love you." Priscilla quickly turned and left Deanna's room closing the door behind her softly before Deanna could ask any more questions about her father.

Priscilla didn't know where to turn. She opened up her laptop, once the children were settled down for the night, and googled hotels in Los Angeles. Several hotels came up and she began her search calling each in turn and asking the same question about whether her husband was listed there.

An hour later she had failed to find Parker booked at any of the hotels. Not knowing what else to do she called the airline to recheck their flights for any news of Parker. The attendant that she had spoken to earlier was on a break so she had to explain herself all over again to another person to no avail. There was still no news about Parker.

Priscilla tried several more times to reach Parker on his cell with still the same results. She knew something was wrong. If he were able to he would answer or at least her call would go to his voicemail.

It would be a sleepless night for her. But Priscilla got ready for bed too and tried to relax by taking a hot bath. Her mind was spinning in all directions trying to figure out what was wrong. She knew that Parker would not make her worry like this unnecessarily. He was a kind and considerate man. He would have called…if he could.

***

Sleep finally came to Priscilla but something wasn't right. She was sitting up in bed talking to someone. Only that someone was just a bright light. She reached out with her hand to touch the light. It was not there but the area around it was warm. She heard a voice calling her name, and Parker's face came into view. He was bathed in the brilliant white light and he had huge wings. He had tears in his eyes, and he spoke in echoey whispers as if he was far away. "Don't be afraid, Priscilla. I am in a better place now. Take care of our children and yourself. I love you and always will."

Priscilla cried out, "Parker, don't leave. Please come back. I love you too," shaking and clearly shocked over what she just heard, Priscilla was now sitting up in bed and wide awake. She looked at the clock – 5:30. She tried to get back to sleep but her mind was in a turmoil. *Did she really see Parker? Was he trying to tell her that he was dead? But what happened to him*? Priscilla lay back and closed her eyes trying to will the light back and unknowingly fell back to sleep. She couldn't believe what she had seen – Parker was now an angel and he had beautiful white wings.

***

Priscilla waited until the next day to call Parker's office in Kelton to see if they had heard from him. They did not know any more than she did about when he would return. In fact they thought he had gone on vacation with the family. Priscilla felt sorry for Parker's secretary, Sonja, who tried to make up every excuse she could for her about his absence. Sonja finally responded that she would call her as soon as she knew anything at all about Parker's whereabouts. Priscilla thanked her and hung up the phone as her hands shook uncontrollably. *What happened to him? Who did he meet out in California?*

Priscilla couldn't just sit there and wonder; she had to find out. The vision she had seen last night of Parker as an angel with wings had told her that he was not coming back. It still didn't explain why or what had happened. Priscilla closed her eyes as the vision came into her mind. She missed him terribly and seeing him in her dream only made her miss him more.

Priscilla wanted to be proactive so she looked through Parker's business mail, contacts and calendar on his desk and his computer files. She even went through all his clothes looking for some clue. There was no mention of a trip to California in any of his correspondence with the store. She even went online to look at his flight and the connecting flight to Kelton to see if there had been any changes. There were no flights booked to California on his computer but there was a flight home for today. *Who booked the flight to California? The airlines didn't have it listed. He must have cancelled it but why? Something was not right! His secretary didn't book the flight to California either. Sonja thought he was going on vacation. Why did he tell her that? Parker must have been doing something illegal or he could have been in trouble somehow. Could he have been buying or selling drugs out in the California? He didn't tell me because he did not want me to worry. Oh, Parker, what were you up to?*

Priscilla didn't know where to turn but knew she needed help. She knew she had to call Parker's parents but dreaded making this call. They would blame everything on her for him running away or whatever he did. It would always be her fault. After all, she was the daughter of a drunk! She was nothing but country scum to them.

Priscilla finally called her in-laws that night after hoping against hope that Parker would call her with a plausible explanation for his disappearance. She waited for the call to be answered.

"Hello," answered Marion Wilfork.

"Hi, Marion, it's Priscilla. I need to tell you"…Priscilla took a deep breath and continued, "Parker went to California on a business trip three days ago and was supposed to come back yesterday but he didn't show up."

"What do you mean he didn't show up?" Marion's voice was sharp and without any compassion.

"I don't know what happened. He hasn't called and was supposed to be home yesterday. There was no word from him about changing planes and I can't reach him on his cell."

"What did you do to him? You must have given him a reason to go away from you," Marion blurted out.

Priscilla was incredulous with this question. She couldn't answer through the tears as she listened to her mother-in-law.

"We will hire an investigator and get back to you if and when we find Parker. He will need to know where Parker went out there and where he stayed."

Priscilla filled Marion in on the details and then said, "Okay, thank you...I...," Priscilla tried to finish but her mother-in-law had already hung up the phone.

Parker's mother reacted as Priscilla had expected. She was angry and worried about her son and blamed Priscilla for his disappearance. *How could she say that it was my fault?*

Priscilla was thankful that her in-laws were going to hire an investigator but the rest of what Marion implied she tried to erase from her mind. Priscilla did not believe for one moment that she had not made Parker happy in every way.

Priscilla called the police next. The police dispatcher told her, "Mrs. Wilfork, we will send out an officer to your home or you can come to the station and file a missing person's report any time. There is nothing we can do until then." It sounded like the dispatcher thought Parker was a runaway husband. Priscilla trembled at the thought. Parker wasn't like that at all. He loved her and their children. She knew he did! *Oh God, I am talking in past tense now. I can't think like that! He is alive! He is coming back! He has to!* Priscilla was doubting that Parker would come back after her dream. She just didn't want to accept that.

Priscilla continued, "But what can I do in the meantime? He is missing. I haven't heard from him and he was supposed to be home yesterday. Can't you help me?"

"Ma'am, I am sorry but we cannot do anything until you file the report. I am sure you will hear from him very shortly. Just sit tight and stay close to home in case he does call. Stop in and file a report or wait until an officer can come there. Then we will see what we can do."

"All right, thank you. I will let you know if he does call me," Priscilla fought back new tears of frustration.

Priscilla did go to the police station later that day and filed the report, not wanting to wait for an officer to come to her. She told the police about the cell phone and the hotels and waited for some sign that they understood that Parker wasn't a runaway husband. She left out the strange vision in her dream for fear that the police would think she was going crazy.

"Thank you, Ma'am. We will do all we can to find your husband. We will let you know if we find out any information at all. If you do hear from him in the meantime please let us know."

"Thank you. I will." Priscilla didn't speak with any officer just another dispatcher at that time. All officers were busy or out on cases at the time.

The following day Priscilla got a call from a police officer. "Mrs. Wilfork, I am Sergeant Wholley. I am the officer on the case of your missing husband. I assure you, Mrs. Wilfork, that I will do all I can to find your husband and will call you back if there is any news at all."

Priscilla thanked the officer for calling and put him out of her mind. She had to let the police do their work and find him but she would keep bugging them until they did. *Did Parker remember our anniversary is in a few days?* He must have had his reasons for not calling or coming home which Priscilla couldn't even begin to fathom. As she had done every day since Parker was missing, she called his cell phone all day long with still no answer. She felt so helpless and didn't know what else to do. Priscilla knew that the police would be doing this also and checking with the phone company about Parker's phone.

***

Priscilla was contacted by her lawyer, Steven Fredrickson, a week after Parker's disappearance. "Priscilla, it's Steven. I need to talk to Parker about some papers he has to sign for the business."

"Oh, Steven, I forgot to call you. Parker has been missing for a week now. He went to California on a business trip and never came home. I have been out of my mind with worry and don't know what to do." Priscilla started to cry and couldn't go on.

"What, he's missing? What happened? I'm so sorry, Priscilla. What do you need me to do? Did you call the police and report this?"

"He went on a business trip to California. Yes, yes, I did call the police and they assured me they would look into it and get back to me."

"Okay, listen Priscilla. I will draw up some papers and look over his will, I am sorry to say this. But I need to look things over about the business too. I will get back to you as soon as I can. Don't worry about anything now. Take care."

"Oh no, I don't think he's dead, Steven. Aren't you being a little premature? You don't have to do that, not yet. He will come home. I know it." Priscilla choked up and had to grab a tissue to blow her nose. She didn't want to share her fears about Parker and her dream but she also didn't want to think of him in past tense...she just couldn't.

"Oh, Priscilla, I am sorry but please let me look into this and see what I can find out. I don't remember Parker saying anything about going on a trip. I will get back to you soon. You will need to make decisions about the store now that he is not here to do that. Okay? I got to go now. Talk to you soon."

An hour later Steven called back, "Priscilla, we need to meet. I am coming over now. This is important and can't wait." Steven hung up before Priscilla could answer.

Within half an hour Steven was at Priscilla's front door. She invited him in and fixed some coffee and pulled out the cake from the freezer she had made for Parker's return and sat down next to Steven on the couch as she waited for him to speak.

"Now Priscilla, I think you need to make a decision about the business. The partners, Redmond Somers and Mark Ford, should be told about Parker's disappearance. Don't you think? They'll want to know what you plan to do with Parker's share. Do you want to keep the business going or do you want to sell out to the partners?" Steven used his business voice to try and keep Priscilla calm.

"Why do you want me to do this? Do you know something that I don't know, Steven? I think it is a little too soon to discuss this, don't you think? I wouldn't even give this any thought because Parker is coming back. I know he would not want to close the business any way. Please keep things running and let the partners know that I will not sell out. I expect my husband to be back soon." Priscilla crossed her fingers behind her back as she said this, doubting now that Parker was ever coming back.

"Okay, I understand. I will handle any legal matters to do with the store and check in with you from time to time if I need a signature on any papers. How are you doing, Priscilla? If there is anything I can do to help you, please let me know."

"Thank you, Steven. I appreciate your concern and help. I am doing as well as can be expected." Priscilla was no longer holding out for a miracle of Parker's safe return.

Shortly after Steven left, one of Parker's two partners, Redmond Somers, called Priscilla to express his concern and that of his partner, Mark Ford, and promised, "Priscilla, we are so sorry to hear about Parker's disappearance. Steven called us. It is so unlike him. I wish we knew something about why he went away so we could help you. He didn't mention anything to us except that maybe soon he was going to take a family vacation. We will do our best to keep the business up to Parker's standards. We will send you a report on how the store is doing. Also, you will continue to get some funds directly deposited into your checking account from the profits each week. I know that is what Parker was doing with his proceeds. If you need anything at all please contact us. Take care and let us know when you hear from Parker."

Priscilla was relieved to hear that the partners would keep the store running as usual and responded, "Thank you both. These funds will help me make ends meet and take some pressure off of selling my crafts for a little while."

Robbie was in the daycare program while Priscilla worked for a few hours each day as an aide and Deanna was in first grade. It was Priscilla's way of keeping close to Deanna in case she needed her mother at school. Priscilla would be able to get a few things done after work and then be back there with Robbie at the end of the day to take Deanna home so she didn't have to take the bus. Priscilla wanted to work to keep her mind active and busy so she didn't have much time to think about things. She was fearful of becoming depressed and of no use to herself or her children.

CHAPTER FOUR

Help Needed

Later that night after getting the kids settled Priscilla made a decision. It was now time to turn to the only family she had, her brother, Merrill. Priscilla didn't want to upset his life by telling him about hers. However, she needed her brother now.

***

Priscilla was lonely growing up until her brother, Merrill, five years younger than she, was born. She helped take care of him and he became like her own child since she devoted every waking moment to him when she got home from school. Priscilla played with him and changed his diapers and fed him and he filled her empty life. Her mother didn't seem to mind her taking over Merrill's care since she was busy working nights and trying to make ends meet. Priscilla and her brother were very close growing up and she watched over him when their parents died.

Priscilla and Merrill's parents had lost contact with their brothers and sisters after they got married and therefore Priscilla and her brother never knew their uncles and aunts and cousins. Her mother had told

Priscilla when she was around ten years old that her siblings did not like her choice of a husband and therefore did not want to have anything to do with Priscilla and her brother.

It took a long time for Priscilla to get over the loss of her parents from the car crash. She thereafter immersed herself in her creative writing and art studies and somehow managed to earn a scholarship to a local college after a lot of hard work and good grades.

Merrill, brilliant as he was, by skipping a few grades in school, was catching up with Priscilla and went to a local college and got a degree, completed in half the time in computer technology and programming and found a good job and a place to live. He had worked two jobs just to get through school since Priscilla didn't make enough with her part-time jobs to put them both through college. He was adjusting quicker than his sister. Merrill got married before Priscilla did and moved away to Georgia with his wife, Carolyn, who he met at one of his jobs. Priscilla didn't get to see Merrill now but kept in touch with him by snail mail and email.

***

Priscilla pulled out her cell and dialed Merrill. Tapping her foot and swaying back and forth she anxiously waited for him to answer. As soon as

Priscilla heard Merrill's voice, she began to cry. "Cilla, is that you? What's wrong, Sis?"

"Oh, Merrill, I should have called you sooner but I was hoping that I would call and give you good news not...," Priscilla once again choked up before continuing. She told her brother what had transpired about Parker, leaving nothing out. After several minutes she sniffled and waited to hear what her brother had to say.

"Oh, dear God, Cilla! I'm so sorry! I don't think Parker would go off like that and not come back. That is very strange. I am sure he will call you soon. In the meantime, did you call the police? What can I do? Do you want me to come up there and stay with you and kids for a while? I can take some time off from work. Carolyn won't mind, in fact, she could use some time away from work too. We would come and stay with you. We haven't seen the kids in a while and Paul would love meeting his cousins. He is nearly eight now. He and Deanna would get along well."

Priscilla pondered over what her brother had proposed. But what she relayed to her brother was completely different.

"Yes, I did call the police. They told me that they would call if they had any news. Merrill, I can't ask you to drop your life and come stay with me. I am surviving alone and will continue to survive. I think this has made me stronger having to do everything without Parker. The children are doing better now. But thank you so much for being there for us. It was cathartic just sharing this burden with you and knowing that you are there if I need you. Thank you, Merrill. I love you, Bro!"

"Yeah, Cilla, I am always here for you! Please call me and let me know if there is anything you or the kids need. If I don't hear from you in a few days I will call you. Okay? Let's keep in touch more than we have and not just by email or snail mail. Is that a deal, Sis?"

"Yes, Bro, it is." Priscilla laughed for the first time in a long time at her little brother's kind words and use of her nickname. No one else called her 'Cilla.'

"Well, listen, Merrill, I will call you back soon, I promise. Say, 'hi' to Carolyn and Paul for me and give them my love. Did I tell you that you are the best little brother a sister could ever have?" Priscilla found herself smiling as she listened to Merrill's response.

"Hey, you bet, Sis! You are the best big sister I ever had!" Merrill chuckled at his own humor smiling broadly himself but quickly becoming somber.

"Thanks, Merrill! Love you! Goodnight and thanks again!"

"No problem, Sis! Love you too! Goodnight!" Priscilla closed her phone and shut off the light as she laid down and promptly fell asleep feeling some peace after talking to her brother.

***

Steven Frederickson sat at his desk thinking over what Priscilla had told him about Parker's disappearance. He couldn't understand why Parker would do something like this. He had known Parker since college and this was not in his makeup to up and leave his wife and children. He just wouldn't do that.

Steven's secretary buzzed him out of his thoughts that he had a call from Los Angeles, California. He quickly picked up the phone thinking it must be Parker. He was just going to say, "Hell, man, what were you thinking?" when a strange voice came on the line, "Counselor Frederickson, I have a proposition for you and need you to come immediately to Los Angeles, California."

CHAPTER FIVE

Weeks turned into months and still there was no word or sign of Parker. He had disappeared off the face of the earth.

Priscilla didn't have any more visions in her dreams but she noticed some things on her bureau and nightstand had been moved. A picture of her and Parker was tipped over, her hairbrush was upside down, her jewelry box was opened and a locket Parker had given her last year for their anniversary was lying opened, and her hand mirror was leaning against a book as if it was standing alone. All this did not make any sense to her. Was Parker trying to tell her something? Maybe he wanted to wish her love on their anniversary from wherever he was now.

Priscilla's in-laws reported they would not stop looking for Parker and had put a private investigator on the case for months now. They had called her once a week to keep her informed of any progress the PI had made. She hoped each time they called that it would be good news and not the usual, "nothing positive to report" from them. Priscilla suffered from bouts of crying and depression after each of these calls. Parker's parents always were cold and distant to her. It was still evident by their behavior that they blamed her for Parker's disappearance.

Priscilla tried Parker's cell phone again as she had nearly every day since his disappearance. This time, however, it didn't even ring. It was clear that his phone was no longer working or had been destroyed. She decided to call the phone company. Maybe they could trace his cell and find him that way. She should have done this sooner but wasn't thinking straight.

Priscilla called her local carrier, identified herself and requested, "I need to speak with a supervisor about tracing my husband's cell phone. I have been unable to reach his cell and want to see if you can help me locate it."

Priscilla waited patiently for the supervisor to come on the line. "Yes, Mrs. Wilfork. I understand that you need to locate your husband's cell phone. You need to give me some information to confirm who you are. What is your home address and phone number? Can you confirm your password for your account? Okay, now Mrs. Wilfork, do you know where your husband last used his cell? When was the last time he phoned you?"

"He hasn't used it in over six months. Well, he hasn't called me anyway. He flew out to California and was supposed to call me from there. But I have been unable to reach him or even get his mailbox to leave a message."

"I see. I will review his calls and see if I can locate it with the GPS tracking. If I can't locate it that way it could be that it is not working any longer."

After an hour on the phone with the local phone carrier Priscilla put down the phone and held her head in her hands. She knew there was nothing she could do. Parker couldn't be traced because his cell phone was not working. In fact, the carrier said they could find no sign of it anywhere in their data bases as being used since his disappearance. Priscilla had to find another way to find Parker.

Priscilla thought the one thing that she was thankful for during this difficult time was that her in-laws had enough funds to keep the private investigator on Parker's case for an indefinite amount of time, something she could not afford to do. In fact her in-laws could keep the PI in alligator shoes and a cashmere coat and driving a Lincoln Continental all over Timbuktu for a very long time. Maybe the PI would have better luck, after all he was from Los Angeles and knew the area well.

The police didn't seem to be having much luck in finding anything out there. When Priscilla didn't hear from the police she called them at least once a week without much luck of any new developments.

The hardest part of Parker leaving her and their children was telling the children that their father would not be coming home. She couldn't even say for sure if he was alive or dead except for the dream.

The children were so young that she decided the kindest thing to do would be to tell them that he had died and gone to Heaven. But she had waited after several months had gone by before she had finally decided to give them this terrible news. It was also to stop the questions from Deanna that she could not answer.

Deanna was very adamant about her father coming home because he had always kept his promises to her. But Priscilla felt she had to try to get their lives back and help her children say goodbye to their father. It was very difficult to keep saying she hoped Parker would call eventually to let them know he was all right. Priscilla was, in a sense, giving up on ever seeing or hearing from Parker again.

Priscilla knew in her heart that he was never coming home especially after the dream. She still, however, needed to know what happened to Parker. It was not easy for Priscilla to accept that he was gone but she also couldn't go traipsing off in search of his whereabouts. She had the children to think of. What would they do if something happen to her too?

Priscilla cringed with the thought of leaving her children with Parker's parents if she went searching for Parker. Deanna and Robbie didn't even know their grandparents. Tran and Marion Wilfork only saw the children after they were born and never came to visit after Parker's disappearance. They didn't even care about the children. This was unconscionable to Priscilla that her in-laws would not want to see their grandchildren once in a while. But, like she mentioned before, they were cold and unfeeling. What else did she expect from them? She was used to being rejected by family since she was a little girl but it wasn't any easier now as a grownup. She would do all she could to protect her children and nurture them so they would always feel loved and wanted at least by her.

***

Police Chief Sangeovese was busy on Parker Wilfork's disappearance for the past several months. He had contacted the Chief of Police in Los Angeles and had relayed all he had on Parker from his wife about his cell phone not working and no sign of him at any hotel in the area. The Los Angeles Police Department promised that they would get right on the case and report back any findings.

Chief Sangeovese had called Parker's cell phone company for any help locating his phone and when it was last used. Mrs. Wilfork had told the police that she had already done this but the phone company would have to give Chief more information than they had given to her.

Strange things had happened but there were still no answers to the disappearance of Parker Wilfork. Something had to give soon.

CHAPTER SIX

A Tough Decision

Priscilla watched Deanna from the doorway of her room. She was busy doing her homework but stopped every few minutes to gaze out the window in deep thought. She had a tough decision to make and now was time to follow through with it.

"Hi sweetheart, what are you doing? Can I talk to you for a moment? I have something very important to tell you." Deanna stopped during her homework, put her pencil down on her desk and looked at her mother expectantly.

Deanna interrupted Priscilla's thoughts by asking, "Is Daddy coming home yet?" This was a question that she had asked her mother every day for nearly a year now. Deanna asked it this time with eager anticipation registering on her face.

"That is what I want to talk to you about. No, sweetie, I am sorry he is not coming home. He is never coming home again. He is in Heaven now with Jesus and all the angels like you learned in Sunday school classes." Priscilla watched her daughter's face for any sign that she understood what she had just told her. She had neglected to take Deanna to church or Sunday school classes since

Parker's death and felt guilty bringing up the subject of angels now. But Priscilla knew she had to.

"No, Mommy, Daddy is not in Heaven. He is coming home soon. He promised me that he would be coming home to bring me a surprise," Deanna stated defiantly and added, "He never breaks his promise."

"I am so sorry, Sweetie, he can't come home. He is in God's House now and watching over you and your brother. He will always love you and watch over you to make sure you are safe from harm." Priscilla tried to explain to her distraught daughter even though she did not have a strong faith herself.

Tears ran down Deanna's face as she continued to deny her mother's words. Priscilla reached out to Deanna and held her tightly in her arms. Priscilla's own tears mixed with Deanna's as they both cried. Priscilla felt not only profound grief but also anger over Parker's loss. *Would she ever know the why or how of his disappearance?*

Robbie was sitting on the floor next to them looking at one of his books, *Sebastian Meets Marvin the Monkey,* when he suddenly looked up and noticed his mother and sister crying. He came over to pat Deanna on the arm and reply in his sweet chatter, "What's matta, Deanna? You cryin?"

Deanna opened her arms to her little brother to embrace him also. Robbie didn't know what was going on but hugged his sister back and smiled at her. Deanna couldn't help but smile back at her sweet little brother. He was too young and innocent to know why his sister was sad. Priscilla looked at her children and felt such grief over their loss of a father but at the same time grateful for them. She would do whatever she could to make their lives happy and try to fill the void that Parker left behind.

Priscilla had tried to answer Deanna's numerous questions but one day she would not be able to answer one very important question. She knew that one day as Deanna got older she would ask what happened to her father and would demand more details. Priscilla dreaded that day for she did not know what had happened to Parker and may never know. But Priscilla felt that she needed to know and would do whatever she could to find out not only for herself but for her children.

***

Priscilla thought over what she had said to Deanna about Heaven. She knew it was time to help her children understand God.

Parker always believed in God and shared his feelings with Deanna as young as she was. He had taught her prayers and sat with her at night while she recited her prayers to God while Priscilla listened from a distance.

A few months before Parker's disappearance Deanna had made her First Communion at age six. This was the only time Priscilla had attended church since the death of her parents when she was seventeen.

Deanna had looked like an angel with her beautiful white dress and veil, white lacy ankle socks and white patent leather shoes. Priscilla held this image of her lovely little girl in her head. Looking at her, who could not believe in angels?

CHAPTER SEVEN

Police Business

The police were working hard on Parker's case during this time. They had never stopped. Chief Sangeovese was on the phone daily in the beginning, and later every week or so, then once a month with the Los Angeles Police Chief. They compared notes and rehashed how this man, Parker, could just disappear so suddenly.

The Los Angeles police had visited the airport and checked the passenger list for Parker's name. They looked at videos at the airport terminal and found Parker leaving the airport and getting into a black limousine. They checked the license plate number which led them to a dead end because it did not exist.

They visited the Hotel Los Angeles where Parker was supposed to have stayed and found no sign of him being there. They checked all other hotels in the area without any success.

The next stop was to see if there was a JemsWorld store and then find the owner for confirmation that Parker met with him. They visited the store and spoke with the owner who denied knowing where

Parker was but did not deny meeting with him. Even if he did admit to meeting Parker how did that prove that he harmed Parker in any way? There was no sign of Parker anywhere in Los Angeles. Besides, being very well connected with the mayor and other local officials, the police had to tread lightly around the manager. They knew something wasn't right but couldn't charge him with anything without proof. They would just have to keep a close watch over him and his dealings for the time being. He would have to slip up eventually.

The LA police had no other leads to follow and knew that after two years the case would be considered a cold case if they could not find any new evidence to keep it open.

Chief Sangeovese knew he had to call Mrs. Wilfork to explain their lack of findings. He punched in her number and waited tapping his pen against his desk in a rhythmic beat.

"Hello."

"Mrs. Wilfork? This is Chief Sangeovese from Leah Mills Police Department. I wanted to get you up to date on your husband's case. I recently spoke with the Los Angeles Police Department. I am sorry to say we still do not have any news about your husband's whereabouts. We have followed whatever leads we could out there but have come to a dead end. If any new evidence comes up we will follow through and check it out thoroughly."

"What? Why are you giving up on finding my husband or what happened to him? What is wrong with you? You can't be serious that you can't even find any evidence? Are you all incompetent? How does that help my children and me? What…what are we supposed to do?"

"I am so sorry, Mrs. Wilfork. We have done all we can. There are no other leads or evidence to keep it actively open. If there are any new developments I will be sure to contact you and reopen the case at a later date."

Chief Sangeovese heard the distress in Mrs. Wilfork's voice and pressed on, "Mrs. Wilfork, I have a question for you. Did you know that your husband's store name is being used out in Los Angeles by a developer? The man in question did not actually admit to meeting your husband but he must have to obtain the rights to the store's name. Have you heard from your lawyer or the partners of the store about this?"

"Well, I did speak with my lawyer and the two owners of JemsWorld a few days after Parker's disappearance. My lawyer, Steven Frederickson said he would call me if he found out any information. Come to think of it, he never did call me back. Do you want me to call him again?"

"No, I will pursue that avenue myself, Mrs. Wilfork. If I find out anything at all I will call you."

Chief Sangeovese was not a cold person and felt Mrs. Wilfork's pain and frustration. He felt helpless in this case. There was no evidence of any foul play to her husband. There was no sign of him going anywhere after the airport. He got into the limo and just disappeared. But the chief's experience told him otherwise. Something did happen to Parker Wilfork but he didn't know what. He did know one thing from similar cases that Parker was most likely dead.

"I don't understand, Chief! Did you do all you could to find him? Please don't give up on this case, I beg you! Please contact me if you have anything new. I need to know what happened to my husband not only for me but for our children. You must understand, Chief."

"Yes, I do. I only wish I could offer you more information. I will call you if there are any new developments. Take care, Mrs. Wilfork. Goodbye."

"Please don't give up, Chief Sangeovese." Priscilla pleaded again before she hung up the phone and dropped her face into her hands and cried tears of frustration. It was over now. There was nothing more the police could do. Parker had disappeared and would never come back.

***

Buzz was circling around the town looking for a place to grab a bite to eat. Boss had given him a job to do but he didn't have to go hungry.

He had been driving by the school and noticed the beautiful blond as she had picked up her two children. Boss didn't say to do anything yet at this time. He would be just observing.

CHAPTER EIGHT

Late summer

"Robbie, hurry up and dress; it is getting late. Do you need some help? I left your clothes on your bed. We need to bring your sister today for the dress rehearsal for her play. Deanna, are you ready yet?"

Each day ran into the next and Priscilla felt as if she couldn't get through another one but somehow she did keep on going. It had been two years since she had lost Parker, so to speak.

Robbie was now four and in preschool and Deanna eight in third grade. The children were doing well in school and settling into their life without Parker.

Deanna was very involved with singing in the choir and she was learning to play the piano. Priscilla had taken her one day to see a play at the local children's theater and Deanna had fallen in love with the idea of acting. There had been a posting at her school for tryouts for the play, *Oliver*. Since that day Deanna had begged her mother to take her to the tryouts. Priscilla finally had broken down and taken her daughter, and much to her surprise, Deanna had been picked for a small part.

Priscilla was thrilled for her and noticed that Deanna was blossoming into a lovely little girl who would one day be a beautiful young woman. Priscilla encouraged her daughter to do all she could do to the best of her ability. Deanna said one day after her rehearsals that she wanted her father to be proud of her. Priscilla told Deanna that her father certainly would be proud, for he was watching over her from Heaven.

Deanna's face was a little puzzled as she asked her mother, "Mommy, how far is Heaven?"

Priscilla found herself at a loss for words. She told Deanna simply, "Heaven is very far away. We cannot get there unless…" Priscilla stopped before she could say-we die.

"Unless what, Mommy?" Deanna looked up waiting for further information from her mother.

"Well, honey, I really do not know where Heaven is. I am sorry. I have never been there. We won't be going there for a very long time, so please do not worry about it, okay, sweetheart?" Priscilla hoped that this explanation or lack of one would suffice for the time being until she was older. She watched Deanna's face for some sign that she was accepting her mother's statement.

Deanna pursed her lips and furrowed her brow as she thought over her mother's words. Priscilla could see Deanna thinking it all over, "Mommy I don't understand why you don't know where Heaven is? Daddy must have known where it is if he is there now? I want to visit him in Heaven one day." Deanna abruptly turned and walked away before Priscilla could respond.

Deanna's one question, 'How far is Heaven, Mommy?' *How could I answer that? Did I even believe in Heaven?*

Priscilla had started taking the children to church more often and enrolled them in Sunday school classes. She was trying but felt she had a long road ahead to believe in God once again. She was doing this for her children.

As Priscilla looked back on that day, their last day together before, well…Priscilla only wished she did believe. Maybe Deanna wouldn't have ventured out to find the answer herself.

CHAPTER NINE

Priscilla sat in the audience with Robbie on her lap as they watched the play, *Oliver*, and waited anxiously for the appearance of Deanna. Priscilla had explained all about the play to Robbie but since he was only four this was a little difficult. Priscilla had told him that it was about many children who did not have families to take care of them or have enough to eat. Robbie had asked in his own innocent way, "Mommy, can I give them my cookies to eat?"

Priscilla couldn't help but feel her eyes well up at this sweet thought from her four-year-old. Robbie was such a darling little boy and was very generous with his toys and sharing his food with her and Deanna, even his favorites, hot dogs, mac and cheese, and grilled cheese sandwiches. But, he could be a handful at times like all little boys. Priscilla felt so much love for Robbie well up inside her as she hugged him tightly.

Robbie squirmed in his mother's lap to get free as he turned to look at the stage where the children were now marching around with soup bowls in their hands. Robbie got excited when he spotted his sister coming onto the stage. Priscilla had to shush him so he wouldn't disturb the rest of the audience. Robbie waved his little hand at his sister to try to get her attention. Priscilla quietly told him that Deanna could not wave back since she was holding a bowl. He accepted that for the time being.

Priscilla and Robbie watched Deanna as she walked forward with her bowl to accept some porridge. She waited in line as the child who played *Oliver* stepped forward to request some more.

The booming voice of the actor who was dishing out the porridge frightened Robbie who held onto his mother's shoulder as he buried his face there. He looked up as the actor pointed a finger at *Oliver* and yelled, "More, you want more!"

Deanna's performance was outstanding as she held her head up high as she looked confident and in her element, acting. Not a peep could be heard as Deanna delivered her few lines. Priscilla held her breath as she listened in awe to her little girl. She felt such pride.

Deanna did a great job and her voice sounded clear and strong along with the older children. She was definitely very talented. It was almost as if she was living this part as a child without a parent.

A wave of sadness passed over Priscilla as she thought of Parker and how much he would have enjoyed seeing Deanna on stage. He had always thought that Deanna was such an actress from the time she began to talk. Deanna was daddy's little girl which made it even harder for Deanna to accept her father's loss. Priscilla knew how much she missed him. For Robbie it was not as difficult since he was so young and didn't remember much about his father. Robbie, in fact, had stopped asking for his father after the first few months of his disappearance.

After the play Priscilla had promised to take Robbie and Deanna out for ice cream at MacIntosh Farm. The summer was passing quickly and Priscilla could feel the air losing the warmth as the days raced toward the fall. The ice cream stand would be closing soon, all the more reason to get one last ice cream cone in.

They had gone to this farm all summer to feed the ducks and geese who flocked to the pond next to the ice cream stand. Parker used to come with them and buy the food for the children to feed the birds. This had been one of his favorite things to do with them. No matter how hard Priscilla tried it always came back to Parker being gone. She realized how sad she felt each time she thought of how much he was missing with their children.

***

Priscilla did whatever she thought was right to do for her children. She remembered after Parker had been missing for six months that she had called the insurance company. Priscilla had pulled out the insurance file from Parker's desk and dialed the number.

"Suffolk Life, how may I help you?"

"Yes, my name is Priscilla Wilfork and I would like to report that my husband has been missing for six months now. I do not think he is coming back. I can't prove just yet that he is dead but the police have been unable to find him. What do I need to do to receive his life insurance?"

"I am sorry Mrs. Wilfork but we cannot do anything about your husband's benefits without a death certificate. There must be proof of his death. The only thing that you could do is to declare him legally dead. But you must have a legal statement from a lawyer that you have done all you can to find him. The only stipulation of this type of statement is that if your husband does suddenly come back you will have to pay back all the money to us with interest. Also, you must wait for seven years before you can declare him legally dead. It could be shorter if he was involved in a catastrophic disaster of natural causes like a hurricane, September 11th disaster or other tragedy as a casualty of war."

"Oh, I don't think anything like that happened where he went. So, you are saying that I need, first of all, to wait seven years before I can legally declare him dead? What do I do in the meantime?"

"I am sorry, Ma'am, but you should talk to your lawyer. There is nothing we can do until you provide the proof of his death."

"I see, but I don't understand. Seven years is a long time to wait with two children to care for."

"Is there anything else I can help you with?"

"No, you haven't helped me with this problem. How can you possibly help me with anything else? Never mind, goodbye." Priscilla hung up before the agent could respond.

It was another dead end for Priscilla. She felt the anger rise up in her at being unable to do anything until she found out what happened to Parker.

CHAPTER TEN

A Ceremony for Parker

Pricilla thought back to the day not too long ago when Parker's parents had held a ceremony for him two years' after his disappearance.

They reported that the PI had not found anything about Parker. In fact, her in-laws suddenly lost contact with the PI in the past year. Priscilla had protested that if they did not have a body, how could they have a funeral? She resignedly told Marion that they would be there for the ceremony.

Priscilla dressed in her one black dress and put the children in their Sunday clothes. She drove up to the Wilfork's home as a chill ran down her spine. She had not been back to their house since their first meeting. That day she would never forget.

Several cars were lined up in the long drive and she found a space behind one and parked. She turned to her children and explained the situation addressing Deanna. "Honey, this is your grandparent's house, Dad's parents. They are having a ceremony for your dad. It is like saying goodbye formerly to him even though we don't know where he is."

"What do you mean, Mommy? What kind of ceremony?"

"It's like going to church to say prayers for those who need our prayers." Priscilla tried in vain to explain what she couldn't understand herself.

"Come on now. Your grandparents are waiting for us to begin the ceremony." Priscilla took her children's hands and moved to the house as the door opened. Marion and Tran stood motionless in the doorway watching them.

The children looked with curiosity at these people and their huge house. Robbie pointed to the tower that rose high above their heads and whispered to Deanna. "Look at that tower, Deanna."

"Well, it is good that you could come, Priscilla," Tran said as he extended his hand in greeting and smiled at his grandchildren.

"How are you two doing? My, you have grown up so fast." Tran rubbed Robbie's head and patted Deanna on the shoulder as he guided them into the house.

Both children looked up at this strange man and watched their mother for any sign that they should not go into the house with him.

"It's okay, kids. Go ahead with your grandfather. I will be right there."

Marion just exchanged silent looks with Priscilla for several seconds before she spoke. "I am …we are happy to see you and the children. It has been a long time. I didn't think you would come."

"Yes, it has. I thought it was the right thing to do even though I do not understand nor do the children." Priscilla didn't know what else to say to this cold woman.

"We need to do this. Parker is never coming back. I can feel it."

"You may be right about that, Marion. I feel that too." Priscilla couldn't believe that she had actually agreed with this woman who was still a stranger to her after all these years.

"Let's go in. The reverend is here and waiting to begin. We will have a luncheon afterward. You and the children are welcome to stay." Marion said this in an unfeeling way as if she really didn't mean it.

"I will see if the children are up to it. Thank you," Priscilla replied back feeling no empathy toward this woman.

The ceremony was short and those attending were strangers to Priscilla except for Parker's siblings who were cool as before toward her. She excused herself as soon as she could and collected Deanna and Robbie quickly.

"Are you leaving already, Priscilla?" Tran asked in surprise.

"Yes, the children are tired and uncomfortable in their clothes and want to go home. It has been a traumatic experience for them and I think it is best that we leave. Thank you for inviting us."

"Oh of course, Priscilla. Let me walk you out to your car," Tran responded in a strained voice.

"Please don't let Marion upset you. She can't help how she is. She holds everything inside and doesn't know how to express her feelings in a kind manner."

"I see, that is what you call it?" Priscilla expressed her disdain for Marion.

"I am sorry but I need to leave. I don't mean to be rude but I find this whole thing uncomfortable. Do you believe I was responsible for Parker's disappearance, Tran?" Priscilla watched Tran's lined and tanned face yet so similar to Parker's.

"I…ah…no, Priscilla. I don't believe that for one minute. But it is difficult for Marion."

"I don't know what to say to change her mind. I loved Parker and he loved me and our children that is all I can say." Priscilla turned and headed back to her car with the children in tow.

Tran called out to her, "Take care of yourself and the children, Priscilla. I'm sorry for everything."

Priscilla couldn't drive away fast enough so she could breathe again. Deanna watched her mother's tormented expressions but didn't say anything.

"Are we going home now, Mommy?" Robbie asked when Deanna wouldn't answer or look at him after he poked her.

"Yes, we are, Robbie. Why don't we pick up a pizza since you are probably getting hungry? We can bring it home and eat it there. Okay?"

"Yeah, I love pizza, Mommy," Robbie cheered.

"Deanna, do you want some pizza?"

"Okay, Mommy," Deanna sighed.

Priscilla looked at her daughter's sad face in the rearview mirror as she drove home.

Priscilla went back to work full-time now as a teacher's aide at Leah Mills Elementary School to keep busy and so she wouldn't dwell on her situation. She put Robbie in daycare at the school after his preschool hours were over until she finished working.

She continued to sell some of her crafts at the local fairs just to keep busy. She did not want to ask for any help from her in-laws. Parker's parents seldom called her anyway and now only to check up occasionally on the children. They told Priscilla to bring the children over to their home for a weekend some time but never gave her a definite date to do it. Deanna and Robbie had only met their grandparents recently at Parker's ceremony and would not like to be away from their mother. It would be like sending them to a stranger's house.

***

Priscilla shook these thoughts out of her head as she held tightly onto Robbie's hand and led him back stage to pick up his sister so they could go for ice cream. Robbie was very excited about going to the farm again. He asked, "Mommy, can I feed the birds?"

"Yes, sweetie pie, of course you can."

Robbie remembered feeding the ducks and geese last year and the year before but he couldn't remember much about doing this with his father. This thought made Priscilla feel despondent.

CHAPTER ELEVEN

Priscilla sat the children at a table closest to the ice cream counter so she could keep a close watch over them as she ordered a cup of chocolate ice cream for Robbie and rocky road ice cream in a sugar cone for Deanna. Priscilla indulged herself and ordered her favorite pistachio ice cream in a plain cone. As Priscilla turned around with her purchases she spotted a man in the distance who looked like he was watching her. It must be her imagination; why would a stranger be watching her? He was probably here with his family and watching over his own children. *What's wrong with me?*

Priscilla hurried over to the children and handed them their ice cream and plenty of napkins as she sat down next to Robbie to help him if necessary. Deanna was watching the ducks and geese, clearly mesmerized by them. She did seem at times to be in her own world. Priscilla worried about Deanna distancing herself. Priscilla knew that Deanna was angry with her for saying that her father was not coming back.

Priscilla came out of her thoughts with Robbie's little voice echoing in her ears, "Mommy, can I have some more chocolate please?" As Priscilla looked down at her son she saw that Robbie's mouth was covered in chocolate and so were his hands. The front of Robbie's shirt was a chocolatey mess too. Priscilla guessed she wasn't paying too much attention for him to have made such a mess of himself. Priscilla pulled a wet napkin out of her bag and cleaned him up as much as she could.

"Well, my little man, I think you have had quite enough for today. Just look at you. I guess you really do love your chocolate ice cream, don't you, sweetheart? I promise we will come back one more time before the stand closes for the season. Ok?"

Priscilla took Robbie's hand and turned to tell Deanna that they would be leaving when she noticed that her seat at the table was empty. Priscilla could hear her heart pounding in her chest and felt the fear creeping into her mind and very soul. Where was she? Priscilla tried to stay calm so as not to frighten Robbie but held tightly to his little hand as she surveyed the area around the ice cream stand and then the pond where there were several children with their parents feeding the ducks and geese.

Priscilla walked around the area and then into the building where there were many customers buying apples and other fruits and vegetables from the clerks. Still there was no sign of Deanna.

Priscilla asked several customers and clerks, "Excuse me, but have you seen a little girl wandering around wearing a denim jacket over a blue jumper, red shirt and red tights and a ponytail with a blue butterfly clip?"

Each person she asked sadly shook their heads and patted her on the arm and promised, "We will keep an eye out for her."

One of the clerks even promised, "I will announce on the loud speaker if she was found. I am so sorry. She may just be mixed in with the other children."

"Thank you. I…I will keep looking in the meantime. Please let me know if you find her. I am at my wit's end right now!" Priscilla took a breath and tried to clear he mind as she continued to look around. She felt her hands shaking, her whole core trembling, and felt like she was under water and drowning. Deanna had disappeared.

Priscilla looked at her watch to see how much time had transpired. They had only been there for an hour and Priscilla had just seen Deanna from the corner of her eye less than a half an hour ago when she had turned to clean Robbie up. Deanna had been finishing up her cone at that time and wiping her own hands and face. Priscilla had noticed prior to that moment that Deanna had a faraway look in her eyes and seemed a million miles away from them.

Priscilla was transfixed and staring all around her. Where could Deanna have gone? She must be around here somewhere. She couldn't have gone far. Priscilla tried to calm herself. Deanna was after all a mature eight-year-old and would tell someone working at the farm if she couldn't find her mother. She wouldn't go with a stranger though. Priscilla had instilled that fear in Deanna at an early age not to trust strangers.

Priscilla suddenly got a sick feeling in the pit of her stomach when her mind replayed the scene of the man in the distance watching her. Oh, my God. He wasn't watching her he was watching Deanna! He.......he could have taken Deanna! *Oh dear Lord, please don't let this be happening. Please, oh God, please!!*

Priscilla called out Deanna's name as she walked around the area of the pond. She scanned all the faces of the children mingling near the ducks and geese.

Some people stopped to ask, "Is everything all right? Can I help you?"

Priscilla was on the verge of tears and clearly upset and told them, "I can't find my daughter. She was just sitting at a table with me eating her ice cream and then she disappeared. I...I don't know what to do. I can't find her!"

One family promised to keep a lookout for Deanna. "We'll look around for her. If we find her we'll bring her back to you here or to the store and then they can call you. What was she wearing?"

Priscilla repeated once again what Deanna was wearing and said, "Thank you. Please let me know if you see her. I'm sick with worry…thank you!"

After more than an hour when there was no sign of Deanna Priscilla ran with Robbie in tow to her car where she deposited Robbie in his car seat. Priscilla rummaged in her bag for her cell phone and dialed the police.

"Leah Mills Police Station, this call may be recorded. Is this an emergency?"

"Yes, yes, it's an emergency! I can't find my daughter? I need help, please hurry!"

"Please Ma'am where are you? Please identify yourself."

"I'm…umm, my name is Priscilla Wilfork. I need some help to find my daughter."

"All right, Ma'am. Where are you and when did your daughter go missing? How old is she?

"I am at MacIntosh's farm stand and she disappeared over an hour ago. Please help me...I don't know what to do."

"Of course, Ma'am. A car is coming your way now. Please stay there and let them know who you are."

"Oh God, thank you...thank you!"

Priscilla couldn't breathe. All the wind had been knocked out of her lungs. She thought she was going to die. She sat in the car for ten minutes which seemed more like an hour before the police finally arrived. Priscilla got out of the car and waved them over to her. Priscilla did not want to leave her son alone for a second. She was so distraught over losing first Parker then Deanna that she couldn't possibly survive losing Robbie too.

As soon as the police detectives pulled into the parking lot Priscilla jumped out of the car and yelled, "Help me please. Over here Officers!"

The police officers drove over to park closer to the woman's car. As they walked up to her they could clearly see how distraught she was.

"Oh my God, thank you, Officers, for coming. I am Priscilla Wilfork; my daughter, Deanna, is missing. I...I don't know what to do? I've looked everywhere and…I can't find her! She was just here…."

"Okay, Mrs. Wilfork, is it? I am Sergeant Furelli and this is my partner, Lieutenant Wholley. Please tell us what happened."

The tears which held off until now gushed out and she sobbed, much to her dismay, as she was trying to explain to the officers what had transpired. They indulged her for a few minutes until she could regain her composure. One of the detectives, Sergeant Furelli, had kind blue eyes. He looked at Priscilla with deep sympathy and patted her arm as he opened the door to her car.

"Please, Mrs. Wilfork, sit down and compose yourself and take a deep breath. We need to know what happened."

Sergeant Furelli, whispered to his partner, "Go get a bottle of water for Mrs. Wilfork. She's going to need it. I will get her statement."

Lt. Gus Wholley grunted and headed into the store to do his partner's bidding.

Priscilla took a tissue out of her pocketbook and wiped her eyes and blew her nose then began again to explain to Sergeant Furelli what she thought had happened to her daughter.

Gus came back and handed the bottle of water to the distraught mother and smiled. "I think you need this, Mrs. Wilfork."

"Oh, thank you, Officer." Priscilla took a quick gulp and continued, "My daughter, Deanna, is eight years old and very bright. Umm, she was wearing a denim jacket over a blue jumper, red shirt and tights and she had her hair in a ponytail with a blue butterfly clip. Oh God, she was eating her ice cream one minute sitting next to me and the next minute she was gone." Priscilla took a deep breath and continued, "I was busy cleaning up my son after he had made a mess of his face eating his chocolate ice cream. But it couldn't have been more than a few minutes that I had turned away from her," Priscilla stated wiping the tears that continued to flow with yet another tissue.

Priscilla also gave Sergeant Furelli a description of the man that she thought had been watching her. She had remarkable recall even in this distressed state of mind. "Sergeant, I saw this man who was about medium height with dark brown hair sticking out of a blue baseball cap and wearing a khaki jacket and black pants watching me. He was standing over near the pond. I thought he was watching me. Dear God, maybe he was really watching my daughter!"

Sergeant Furelli listened and took notes on a small pad that he had pulled out of his breast pocket. He nodded and hummed at different times during Priscilla's explanation before finally looking up at her. He had registered the name and connected it to the disappearance of this woman's husband. He wondered if the disappearance of the man's child now had anything to do with the father's disappearance.

"Mrs. Wilfork, I assure you we will find your daughter, Deanna. My partner, Lt. Gus Wholley, and I will look around the farm and ask some of the workers here if they saw a little girl wandering around. Please go home now with your son. How old is he, three or four? He looks like he is getting a little antsy waiting for you. I have a son about his age too. He keeps me hopping. We will call you as soon as we know anything. I know the waiting part is very hard. Please try to rest and take care of yourself and your son. Do you want me to drive you home, Mrs. Wilfork? Are you okay to drive?"

Sergeant Furelli was about her age, Priscilla thought, but he appeared to be much older by his mannerisms and patient nature in handling delicate situations like missing children. He seemed very concerned and compassionate.

"I can't leave here. What if Deanna comes back and looks for me? No, thank you Sergeant Furelli, I will be fine." Priscilla stared with a glazed look at Sergeant Furelli and then turned to her son in the back seat of her car who was now very squirmy and getting clearly impatient. "Robbie, please sweetie, I promise we will be going home soon. I know you are getting restless and tired." Priscilla leaned in and kissed Robbie on his cheek.

Sergeant Furelli emphatically stated, "Please Mrs. Wilfork. We will not leave here until we have some news for you. We will bring Deanna home as soon as we find her."

***

Sergeant Furelli walked back to his car and standing next to it used the mike on his shoulder to report in to the station about his findings in the lost little girl case. He didn't want to report back to the station in front of Mrs. Wilfork. He felt a fear building up in the pit of his stomach just thinking of the possibility of a kidnapping of this little girl. By the sounds of what the mother had told him, the man who Mrs. Wilfork thought had been watching her may have actually been watching her daughter. When Mrs. Wilfork was cleaning up her son after he had eaten his ice cream the man may have lured Deanna away from the table somehow and taken her away with him. The other alternative was that Deanna had just wandered away and would turn up on her own. This alternative was much more pleasant to think about but not plausible.

Sergeant Blake Furelli had only been on the Leah Mills Police force for five years now and had already made Sergeant. He was going to be thirty in another month but felt a lot older. Each time he had to work on a lost child case he felt as if he aged ten years. He knew what the odds were for finding this child and the longer she went missing the higher the odds were that they would not find her alive.

The police had been lucky so far finding several lost kids over his five years with the Leah Mills Police. Most of the kids had been found out wandering around or playing in the woods or at a friend's house except for one little boy, Peter Carter, who was six years old at the time of his disappearance. Peter had been missing for over six weeks now. Blake was not giving up on finding him alive yet. Now with Priscilla's daughter, Deanna, eight years old, missing too, Blake found himself thinking about little Peter Carter. Blake promised Peter's parents as he had done to Priscilla that he would find their son and daughter prospectively.

Blake planned on looking up the report of Parker Wilfork and compare it to Deanna's disappearance. Maybe somehow they were connected.

Also, Blake would look over the missing boy's case and compare it with Deanna's report. He had to cover all bases thoroughly.

Peter Carter had been taken from his backyard. His mother went into the house to answer the phone and when she came back Peter was gone.

Blake had a son of his own, Matthew, who was three. Blake knew what it felt like to almost lose a child. Blake's wife and son had been in a car accident when Matthew was just a few months old which took the life of his wife. Loriann, had been crushed in the front seat from a head-on crash with a drunk driver. Luckily Blake's son was in the baby carrier car seat and strapped facing backward. The front passenger seat had miraculously cushioned his son keeping him unharmed from the crash.

It never failed; every time Blake came in contact with the family of a missing child he felt their pain as he did now. He watched Mrs. Wilfork start up her car then wave to him and drive away. He had promised her that he would call her. He would keep his promise but go a step further by going to visit her in person to report his findings. Hopefully he would have good news for her. Mrs. Wilfork's face came into his head as he thought about what she had said and how she had cried. Her eyes were sky blue, red rimmed now from spent tears, and she had long blonde hair, a little disheveled, and a lovely angelic face. She had looked at him with such desperation and fear in her eyes. He told himself that this was his job and that he should not get personally involved with this woman. But he could still smell her perfume, flowery, sweet and spicy all at the same time.

***

"Hey Blake, are you with me? What is the matter with you? You look like a love sick puppy. She was quite a looker, huh, Blake?" Lieutenant Gus Wholley was pushing sixty now and was looking forward to retiring in a few years or less. He was Blake's superior but treated him more as an equal. He even thought of Blake Furelli as his son. They had become close over the past five years. Gus always looked out for Blake, even though he knew that Blake could take care of himself. Though Blake was a young man, he was wise beyond his years. The tragedy of losing a loved one can do that to a man. Gus observed the concern on his partner's face about the lost little girl. Gus knew that Blake was attracted to Mrs. Wilfork as soon as his partner had set eyes on her. Who wouldn't be? Priscilla Wilfork was beautiful and in distress. Two things that always hooked a man like Blake.

"I am fine, Gus. Let's get moving and find this little girl, ok? Keep the remarks to yourself, old man. This is serious stuff now. You can rag on me later, partner." Blake smiled but not with his eyes as he looked at Gus.

"No problem, Blake. I was only kidding you as usual. I want to find this little girl as much as you do. Let's go talk to some people around here. Maybe someone noticed this man taking Deanna away to his car."

Gus was about twenty or so pounds overweight. Gus tried to move quickly but his knees, achy from arthritis weren't cooperating.

He was definitely feeling old today as he watched his younger and physically fit partner moving swiftly on young knees without a hitch through the crowd of people. Sometimes Gus felt like the underling the way Blake liked to take over all their cases. Gus really didn't mind after all he was on his way out and Blake was just beginning his career as a policeman. Gus knew that Blake respected him and looked up to him because of his experience but Gus thought he just might have to remind the young whippersnapper about a thing or two from time to time.

Well, a job had to be done, Gus thought determinedly as he pushed himself forward on his creaky old legs following Blake as he stopped to speak with individual people and groups about whether they had seen the little girl and/or the man.

Every minute counted now. He only hoped and prayed they were not too late to find this little girl.

CHAPTER TWELVE

Priscilla

Priscilla drove in a daze not seeing or hearing anything around her. The mind does mysterious things to a person. She somehow got home and was surprised about that fact. Priscilla felt like she had died and her body was moving on its own accord without her heart or soul, just an empty shell.

Priscilla had to snap out of this for her son's sake. Poor Robbie had fallen asleep in the back seat and Priscilla tried not to wake him as she unbuckled his seat belt and carefully lifted him out of the car. Robbie must have become exhausted from the all stress. At least one of them would get some rest she thought as she looked at Robbie's peacefully sleeping face.

Priscilla changed Robbie and cleaned him up as best she could without waking him and then put him down for a nap. She knew that he would sleep at least a couple of hours. He still took his naps when he had a busy day. For this Priscilla was very thankful since she couldn't deal with anything extra right now. She needed some quiet time to think through what had transpired. Priscilla was sick with worry about Deanna and where she could be and what she was going through. She must be very frightened.

Maybe she should call her in-laws and tell them what happened. But on the other hand Deanna just might be found by the police. The police were very concerned and seemed very competent especially the younger officer, Sergeant Furelli. The older gentleman's name sounded very familiar to her. The last time Priscilla spoke with the police was when her husband had disappeared and at that time an officer called her back…. Wholley, yes that was his name. He was very nice on the phone and told her that if any news came up that he would call her right away. He had called her regularly without any new developments but just to check in and let her know that the police were still working on the case. Now Chief Sangeovese reported that Parker's case was considered closed until some new evidence was discovered.

Oh Parker, where are you? Please come to me in my dreams again. I need you now more than ever. Where is Deanna? Are you connected somehow? Please God help me!

Priscilla found herself thinking about God for the first time in a very long time. She always felt that He had abandoned her way back when her parents were killed in the car accident. He didn't hear her prayers then and let them die. Would He hear her prayers this time about her daughter's disappearance?

Priscilla didn't know what else to do. She had to do something. She just couldn't sit here without trying to pray. Priscilla found herself on her knees; hands clasped tightly together and head down as she tried to think of a prayer to recite. It had been so long since she had prayed. She had just started taking the children to church. Parker used to take the children to church on Sundays and Priscilla always came up with excuses to stay home saying that she needed to clean and cook and do other jobs around the house. Parker knew the real reason Priscilla didn't go but never mentioned anything to her about it. He was always so patient and kind and thoughtful of her feelings.

Priscilla thought hard and started her prayer, "Dear Lord, please hear my prayer. I lost my husband and life came to a halt for a time but I somehow continued to go on for our children. But now, Lord, my daughter is missing and I feel as if I cannot go on without her but I know I must for my son. Please help me find her and bring her back to me safely. Please do not let anyone harm her in any way. Please send a guardian angel down to watch over Deanna. Dear God, I beg of you!"

"I know I haven't always been the best person that I could be. But I have been angry over my parent's death. You didn't hear my prayers! After my father died, I begged you to let my mother live. Why, God, why did you let her die?"

"I know I should be more forgiving and kinder and friendlier to others but I guess I am afraid of getting hurt if I open up to others. Please help me, Lord! I don't know what to do or who to turn to. I need you! Please God, hear my prayer!"

Priscilla didn't know how long she had been on her knees praying but the ringing of the phone brought her back. When she got up to answer it she realized her legs had fallen asleep and she couldn't trust them to hold her up. Priscilla crawled over to the phone and used the wall to hold onto as she raised herself up off the floor.

She nearly dropped the phone as she was groping to pull it off the wall and trying to keep steady on her numb and tingling legs at the same time. Priscilla felt groggy as if she had fallen asleep while praying but managed to say hello to the caller.

"Mrs. Wilfork, this is Sergeant Furelli. I promised I would call you back with any news. Unfortunately, we haven't found your daughter but we do have some information that I would like to share with you. Can I drop by to see you shortly?"

"Are you all right Mrs. Wilfork?" Blake's voice registered deep concern as he waited for a response from her.

"I...I...I'm okay. What...what did you say about Deanna? Do you have some news for me?" Priscilla's voice choked up as she braced herself for the worst news.

"Please Mrs. Wilfork; I assure you we do not have any bad news for you. It might be considered promising news. I would like to come see you and talk to you about this. Ok? I am not far from your house and I could be there in less than ten minutes."

"Okay, yes, of course please come over. I need to hear some good news and need to know what you found out. I will put on a pot of coffee for us."

Priscilla felt as if she needed to keep herself busy or she would go crazy about not knowing what the police found so she prepared the coffee. She guessed the detective thought it would be better to tell her in person, Priscilla thought. What could it be? Sergeant Furelli promised it wasn't bad news. *Dear God please give me strength to deal with whatever I need to.*

CHAPTER THIRTEEN

"Do you know what you are doing, Blake? It looks like you are becoming too close to this case for your own good." Gus shook his head at his partner's ignorance of his feelings for this woman, the mother of the lost girl. Gus had just listened to Blake's conversation with Mrs. Wilfork.

"Listen Gus, I am only trying to show a little consideration for Mrs. Wilfork; she has been through a lot in the past. I feel the disappearance of her daughter might put her over the edge. You do remember that her husband disappeared over two years ago and was never found or heard from again. You were the officer on the case, or did you forget? Don't you think that is enough for any person to handle? But losing a child is the worst! She could lose it altogether. She has a son you know, about the same age as my Matthew. I know I almost lost it when Loriann died and if I had lost Matthew too...I...well, I don't think I would have wanted to go on living." Blake sighed deeply as he pulled over to the curb and dropped Gus off at the station before going on his way to see Mrs. Wilfork.

Gus waved and watched Blake as he drove away. All Gus could do was shake his head and sigh. He knew Blake was a goner. This woman had gotten to him more than his partner realized.

As Blake drove the short distance to the Wilfork's house he thought over what he and Gus had found out. Gus and Blake had sat in the police car for several minutes comparing notes after they had each spoken to several people at the farm store and ice cream stand. They had received a lot of 'No, I didn't notice the little girl or the man you are referring to' before a woman and her two children had come to talk to them. That's when it got a little strange. They hadn't known what to make of the strange story the mother and her son and daughter had told them. But Blake felt it was something positive and a reason to tell Priscilla. It just might make her feel better or she may think he was crazy. As he pulled up to Priscilla's house he already thought he was crazy even to consider such a thing. Blake hoped that Priscilla had an open mind about things like this he thought as he exited the car and walked up to her front door.

Blake knocked once and the door opened so abruptly that his hand was still poised as a closed fist. Standing in the doorway was a vision, a more beautiful sight he had never seen. Even with her hair in disarray and her eyes red from crying, Priscilla was beautiful in his eyes! Blake found the air knocked out of his lungs as he had stopped breathing and stood there like a statue just staring at this vision of loveliness. They had both stared at each other for several seconds before Priscilla spoke first.

"Sergeant Furelli, I am sorry for startling you like this. I was anxious to find out what you had to tell me. I apologize if I caused you any alarm. Please come in. The coffee is ready and I have some cake too. I thought that you might like something to eat while we talk. It is my own recipe and a lot better for you than fast food." Priscilla led the way into her kitchen looking almost as dazed as Blake who was finally recovering.

"Well, thank you, Mrs. Wilfork. I appreciate the coffee and the cake too. I agree we police eat too much fast food for our own good." Blake replied as he settled down at the table and fixed his coffee and took a bite of the cake before beginning his story.

Blake could tell that Priscilla had enough of the chitchat and wanted him to get on with it. So he began to explain that he and his partner, Gus, had walked around and checked every possible hiding place at the farm that a little girl could use.

Blake continued to explain as carefully as he could, "We looked everywhere possible for Deanna and even asked some of the neighbors on all sides of the farm if they had seen a little girl wandering around their yards."

"Then we talked to as many people as we could who may have seen Deanna and this man or if they were seen together. We had almost given up getting any information from the people walking around the store and stand when a woman and her two children came over to us." Blake stopped and took a deep breath before continuing. He watched Priscilla's face showing her anxiety but some curiosity at the same time as she expectantly waited on Blake's every word.

"I don't know how to explain what the woman and her children told me. I don't know if you will believe it either but please hear me out. You can make your decision later about whether to believe this or not."

Priscilla was getting more anxious as Blake tried to explain in a convoluted way what he was having a very difficult time saying. She didn't know what to think about this. But she wished Sergeant Furelli would hurry up and get to the point.

"What is it Sergeant? You have me very confused and anxious. Please just tell me what it is so I can make up my mind whether to believe it or not. I don't think I can stand guessing what you are going to say much longer," Priscilla's brow was deeply furrowed as she looked at Blake's handsome, troubled face.

"Ok, I am sorry for making you wait. I am having a hard time trying to figure out how to explain this phenomenon. I made the woman repeat herself three times before I began to believe she saw what she had described to me. The children also corroborated her story. The girl was ten and the boy was eight."

"Sergeant, please go on. Are you trying to drive me crazy? Just tell me, please. I need to know whatever it is if it involves Deanna," Priscilla beseeched in a shaky voice with a fierce look on her face.

"I…well…this woman, about your age, came over to Gus and I as we were getting ready to head back to the station. She looked very pale indeed and was visibly trembling. She held tightly onto her two children's hands as she began to tell us her story." Blake pulled out his notepad to refer to his notes.

"This woman said she saw a little girl at the pond talking to a man in a khaki jacket and black pants and blue baseball cap. She said that the little girl took the man's hand and walked away to his car. She didn't think anything about it because she thought it was the little girl's father. She was about to turn away when her children simultaneously called out to her to look at the car as it was pulling away from the farm. She said she couldn't believe it if she hadn't seen it with her own eyes. She told me she wasn't crazy and didn't normally believe in ghosts and spirits. She said there was a man, but not quite a man – he was all in white and he had wings. This man, all in white, had giant wings and he was flying alongside the car looking in at the little girl. He was talking to her and she was smiling back at him. This woman heard Deanna call out, 'Daddy.' The woman and the children were excited and believe what they saw was an angel. They said they thought this was Deanna's guardian angel."

Blake closed his pad and looked over at Priscilla who was crying silently with her hands covering her mouth. He noticed that her shoulders were shaking and he reached across the table and handed her his handkerchief.

Priscilla took it gratefully and wiped her eyes and blew her nose. She nodded at Sergeant Furelli and tucked his handkerchief into her pocket for later use. She was visibly in shock and finally could talk after a few minutes of clearing her throat.

"It must be my husband, the angel I mean. I know he must be dead. Something happened to him. He is with Deanna watching over her. She is safe. I feel it; she is safe. He will bring her back home. I know he will." *Oh, God heard my prayers and sent the angel ahead of my prayers. Thank you God, watch over Deanna and bring her back to me. Have Parker bring her back to me.* Priscilla sobbed noisily now after her outburst of relief.

In a comforting tone, Sergeant Furelli stated, "I am sure your husband is watching over Deanna and so is God. But we will continue to look for her and do whatever we can to bring her back to you. In the meantime take care of yourself and your little boy. I will keep in touch. Are you all right if I leave you alone, Mrs. Wilfork?" Blake was reluctant to leave her in this state but Priscilla did seem more relieved and less anxious now.

"Yes, I will be fine, Sergeant. Please call me Priscilla. I would appreciate it if you could give me that woman's name and phone number. I would like to thank her for this news. I am truly grateful to you too for what you have done and for sharing this woman's words with me. I know you didn't have to tell me this. But I am thankful, believe me. I feel hope now about getting Deanna back. I can finally let go of my husband too. I have wondered for over two years why he did not come back to us or even call to tell us why he couldn't come home. I tortured myself over it. It almost destroyed my daughter too. She has been so despondent the whole time. She hasn't accepted his disappearance either. I still need to know what happened to him but at least now Deanna will be happy that her father has not forsaken her. He has come back as her guardian angel."

"Thank you, Sergeant Furelli, for everything. I promise to get this handkerchief back to you after I wash it, that is. Please keep in touch with me if you hear any more about Deanna's whereabouts and if someone else has seen her and her guardian angel."

No sooner did Priscilla stop talking but the tears started flowing copiously again. She again reached into her pocket for the detective's handkerchief to try to staunch the flow.

"Mrs. Wilfork, I mean Priscilla, I cannot give you the woman's name or phone number. I'm sorry. That is privileged information. Even giving you her testimony about seeing your daughter is against standard procedure. But I know how much you needed something to believe in. I felt that it was my duty to give you this information for that reason. I hope you understand. Please take it easy now. I think your son is waking up. I just heard him call you. I will let myself out and talk to you soon. Goodbye Priscilla."

Blake pushed himself away from the table after a last quick sip of his already cold coffee and taking the rest of his cake with him left the room. He let himself out the front door and walked slowly back to his car. Blake popped the remaining piece of cake into his mouth as he licked his lips. It was the best cake he had ever had, much better than any greasy fast food.

Blake had felt some relief observing Priscilla as the anxiety had left her face leaving her brow smooth and her eyes sparkling. She truly believed what the woman had said about the angel. Blake found himself believing a little in spite of the insanity of it all. *Were angels real? Do we all have guardian angels watching over us?* Police really need guardian angels with all the dangers we come across. I hope my guardian angel is keeping alert and watching over me, Blake mused.

Blake remembered the guffaws from Gus as they had listened to the woman's tale. Gus had made the crazy gesture with his finger pointing to his head after they got back to the car. Blake couldn't believe it at first but then he found himself leaning toward the woman's explanation a little more each time he thought about it. If the woman had gotten a description of the car or the license plate they would be in a better place right now. The angel was such a shock that that was all she saw.

This case also made Blake think back to his wife's accident. Blake truly believed at that time that his son's guardian angel was there with Matthew during the accident. Maybe that is the reason Matthew survived. Blake was also relieved big time that Priscilla was accepting this as fact and that she now had some hope back in her life. He knew what hope felt like. It could keep you alive and going strong. Without hope, life was not worth living.

Also, you need a large amount of faith too. Blake found his hope and faith each time he looked at his son.

CHAPTER FOURTEEN

"Well my little man, did you sleep well? Let's make a trip to the potty and then I will make both of us some dinner. Ok, Robbie?" Priscilla felt as if a weight had been lifted off her chest and now she could breathe more deeply without pain. She knew that Deanna was safe with her father watching over her. Priscilla was sure that Parker, the guardian angel, would find a way to get their daughter back home safely.

Priscilla looked to Heaven and silently prayed, "Thank you, God, for sending Parker to watch over Deanna. Thank You for hearing my prayer. I am truly grateful to You. I promise from now on I will go to church regularly."

Priscilla watched her son as he finished up in the bathroom zipping up his big boy pants and then washing his hands. Robbie smiled up at his mother and took her hand as they walked out to the kitchen together to prepare their dinner.

"Mommy, where is Deanna? Did she go out to play without me?" Robbie innocently asked. He wasn't aware of what had transpired at the farm. Priscilla was thankful that she didn't have to tell him either. She planned to tell him that Deanna was staying at a friend's house for a little while. Priscilla had to have an excuse for Deanna's absence however long it took for her guardian angel to bring her home. But at the same time could she depend on this angel? Priscilla was still distraught and prayed daily that He would help not only the angel but the police find Deanna.

Robbie accepted his mother's explanation and then asked for another glass of milk to wash down his food. He had eaten all his chicken and rice and had only left a few green beans and was now looking for dessert.

Priscilla cut a slice of cake that she had made that morning and put it on a plate in front of Robbie. He looked at it and poked it a bit before trying a piece. Robbie was not the adventurous sort when it came to food. But if he liked the look or smell of some food he would try it. Evidently he liked the smell of cinnamon and the nuts all over the top of the cake because he ate every bite.

Priscilla ate her salad and grilled chicken and sipped her coffee as she looked out the window and watched the sun slowly setting in the west. She was daydreaming about Parker flying around on his newfound angel wings. She wished she could see that. He would be quite a sight, she thought.

Robbie's little voice brought her out of her thoughts. "Mommy, can I go play in my room with my cars and trucks?"

"Of course, sweetheart, but first let me clean you up. You have sugar all over your mouth and your hands are sticky from the cake. You liked Mommy's cake, I see. You are wearing it all over your lap too." Priscilla wiped her son's hands and face and noticed as he smiled at her how very much he resembled Parker. Robbie was a miniature version of him. It made Priscilla's heart skip a beat just to look at him.

"You can go play in your room until I finish my dinner. Ok, sweetheart? I will be finished soon then I will give you a bath and get you in your PJs. There is a special Disney show on tonight and I know you will love it. We can watch it together. Ok?"

"Ok, Mommy. Is it the one about the fairy princess and the mean monster?" Robbie made a scary face, his version of a mean monster.

Priscilla couldn't help but laugh as she watched her son's face contort into a myriad of expressions. "I don't know if there is a monster in it but we will find out, won't we. I am sure it is not too scary. But as long as you hold my hand I will be fine. Ok Robbie?"

"Don't be scared Mommy I will protect you from the monsters," Robbie smiled as he ran off to play in his room.

Priscilla smiled to herself as she thought of how fortunate she was to have her children. She could not have survived after Parker had disappeared without them. Now she would survive again this time, she was sure of it, until Deanna came back. She was putting all her trust in God and His guardian angel, Parker, who God had assigned to her daughter. She knew God wouldn't let anything happen to Deanna. Priscilla found herself praying silently again to God that it wouldn't be very long before He would send Deanna safely back to her.

Priscilla was washing the dishes and cleaning up the kitchen when the phone rang. She wiped off her hands on the dish towel and reached over for the phone on the wall a couple of feet away.

"Hello. Oh, hello, Sergeant Furelli. Yes, I'm fine. Thank you for asking. No, you didn't disturb my dinner. I just finished. Robbie is doing well too. He is playing in his room. Fortunately, he doesn't know what's going on. He thinks that his sister is staying at a friend's house. I thought it would be best if he didn't know that she was missing. He is too young to comprehend what that means. I want to thank you again for what you told me. It gave me such hope and relief. I know Deanna is safe and will be home soon."

"Well, I am glad I could help. I promise you we will do all we can to expedite getting her back to you safely. I am glad to hear that Robbie is doing okay. He is a sweet little boy. I think you are right not to tell him too much. He is too young and innocent to understand this situation. I am sure you won't have to tell him anything because Deanna will be home before he really begins to miss her. In the meantime if you need me for any reason or if you need to talk about this, you can reach me here at the station. Well, have a good night, Priscilla. Take care."

"Thank you, Sergeant. Good night." Priscilla put the phone down after writing down the police station number. She couldn't believe how thoughtful and kind Sergeant Furelli was being. She had never met any police that were as sympathetic or kind. She pictured the officer's face in her mind and found herself feeling warm all over. He was tall with dark blonde hair and blue eyes, an exceptionally handsome man and about her age she thought.

What am I thinking? He is an especially nice man and I am sure he is kind to everyone he comes in contact with. That is his job. Priscilla scolded herself for putting more into Sergeant Furelli's kindness and attention than was necessary.

Priscilla looked around her tidy kitchen to make sure everything was in order before shutting off the light and going to Robbie's room to get him into the tub for his nightly bath.

Later on, she got ready for bed and her thoughts were always of Deanna as she prayed that her daughter was safe wherever she was and that no harm would come to her.

CHAPTER FIFTEEN

"Hey Furelli, what are you still doing here? Isn't it time for you to go home? Your son must be waiting for you to pick him up at the sitter's," Chief of Police Angelo Sangeovese retorted as he stood looking down at Blake sitting at his desk as Sergeant Furelli had just gotten off the phone with Priscilla.

"Oh, yeah, Chief. I was just finishing up and getting ready to leave. My neighbor takes care of Matthew and she's used to me being late. But I do want to spend some time with Matthew before he goes to bed. He does need me more since his mother is gone."

"Have any luck getting info on that little girl?" Chief watched Blake's face which appeared a little flushed.

"Um, not really, Chief, but will keep on top of things," Blake didn't meet the Chief's watchful eye as he answered. He felt the Chief was looking at him in an odd way which made him a little uncomfortable.

"I will leave my latest notes on your desk. Okay, Chief, I will be heading out." Blake shut off his computer and closed and locked his desk drawers.

Well, get going, Sergeant," Chief reiterated.

"Yeah, good night, Chief. See you at 7:00 am."

Blake felt as if his face was red. He had been thinking about Priscilla when the Chief's voice took him out of his reverie. Blake found himself very attracted to Priscilla. He couldn't stop thinking about her and how she looked when she was relieved after he told her the woman's story that Deanna was being watched over by the guardian angel as such. Priscilla's blue eyes had gotten so bright and beautiful and her face had a luminescence that only angels have. Oh boy, he knew he had it bad! What was he thinking? He couldn't get involved with this woman no matter how beautiful and angelic she was.

Blake grabbed his coat from his locker and rushed out the door to go pick up his son. He was looking forward to this time of the night when he could spend some time with his son and listen to Matthew talk about his day at preschool. Matthew was doing surprisingly well at school, loved his teacher and had plenty of friends. Matthew had recently asked his father to come to school in his uniform for show and tell. He was very proud that his father was a policeman. Blake couldn't help but smile at the sweet way Matthew had asked him to come to school, "Daddy, can you come to my school next week? We are doing show and tell and you could tell everyone you are a policeman. Can you, Daddy, please?"

Of course, Blake couldn't refuse his son anything. He told Matthew, "I would be very happy to go to your school and talk to your classmates."

Blake remembered how Matthew's face had lit up with his biggest smile and his eyes crinkled up at the corners as he hugged his father fiercely after Blake had agreed to go. Blake's eyes had misted up at his son's exuberance. Matthew was Blake's whole world and he thanked God every day for sparing his life. He missed his wife terribly but was thankful at the same time that he did not lose both of them. Blake didn't think he would have been able to go on living.

Matthew was a highly intelligent little boy of four. Blake knew that Matthew's IQ had to be way off the charts. He had starting speaking shortly after he started walking at a year old. Matthew was putting together sentences at two that were worthy of a much older child. His intelligence had blown Blake away. Loriann had an extremely high IQ and had been at the top of her class when she graduated from law school. She had been an excellent lawyer and a wonderful wife and mother too. Matthew must have inherited his mother's high intellect for Blake did not graduate at the very top of his class at the police academy but did well enough.

Blake found himself thinking back to the day Loriann and he had gotten married and how beautiful she had looked in her white dress with her hair up accented with white flowers. They were so much in love. He still couldn't believe that she had been dead now for almost four years. Loriann would have been so proud of their son and how he had grown to be such an adorable and intelligent little boy.

Blake had told Matthew all about his mother when he was two. Matthew wanted to see pictures of his mother and kept one of these pictures next to his bedside so he could look at it. Matthew also told his mother how much he missed her and loved her every night. Blake had told Matthew that his mother was watching over him from Heaven to make sure he was always safe. Matthew had smiled when he heard this and looked up to see if he could see his mother watching him. Matthew was a very happy and contented little boy and never seemed upset about anything. He was growing up to be a stable and secure little boy, thanks to God thought Blake.

Blake's thoughts as he got Matthew ready for bed was how blessed he was. He only hoped and prayed that he would be able to bring both missing children back safely to their distraught parents. He believed that somehow Parker's disappearance was connected to Deanna's.

CHAPTER SIXTEEN

Deanna

Deanna had walked over to see the ducks and geese at the pond at MacIntosh's farm stand. She wanted to get closer to her father by doing all the things that he had done with her when he was still with them. She felt angry all the time with her mother for sending her father away. She didn't understand why he had to go away. Why didn't he want to come back to see her? He had promised her he would come back.

Deanna fell asleep every night since her father left with his picture under her pillow. It was the picture her mother had taken of them feeding the ducks at MacIntosh's. She remembered that day so clearly as if it was yesterday. She remembered that her father had said he would always be there for her no matter what. He had given her a surprise early birthday gift since he said he couldn't wait to see her face and wanted to share it with her alone.

She remembered how excited she had felt and her heart was skipping a beat as she tore off the paper and opened the little box. Her eyes had lit up when she saw the beautiful blue butterfly hair clip. Deanna had hugged her father tightly, kissed him and thanked him excitedly. He knew how much she loved butterflies.

When Deanna was only eleven months old and beginning her first steps her father told her that he had taken her outside to walk holding onto her little hands as he guided her over to the flowers along the wall at the back of their modest house. Her father had wanted Deanna to see something special and had pointed out the butterflies as they flitted from one flower to another. Deanna didn't remember that first time but she did remember all the other times he took her outside to watch the butterflies. She fell in love with their beauty and the graceful way they flew around the flowers. She especially liked the blue ones and now she had her own special blue butterfly which she wore every day since then.

Deanna was so busy daydreaming about her father and her butterfly hair clip that she didn't see or hear the man standing next to her right away. She turned her head toward him as she heard him ask her a question.

"Who are you looking for little girl? Would you like to see something special? Do you like butterflies, little girl?" The man had noticed the little girl caressing the butterfly hair clip in her hair.

The man looked familiar to Deanna and she thought maybe he was a friend of her father's that she had seen before. *What did he say? He said exactly what my father said to me that day about seeing something special and he knows I like butterflies. He must know my father. Maybe he knows where my father is*, she thought silently.

Deanna looked up at the man in the khaki jacket and black pants. She responded, "I am looking for my father. Do you know where he is?"

The man nodded at Deanna and reached out his hand to her. Deanna took it and walked with the man to his car at the far end of the lot. He opened the door and put her in the back seat and attached her seat belt. He locked all the doors before slowly driving out of the parking lot of MacIntosh's farm stand.

***

The man could hear the little girl talking animatedly to herself. She was a strange one but a lovely little girl at that. He heard her say, 'Hi Daddy' which he thought was weird since she said she was looking for her daddy. He looked back at her to make sure she was alone. She was alone but she had a beautiful smile that lit up her whole face as if she knew something that no one else did.

As the man pulled out of the parking lot onto the main street he noticed a little boy and girl standing next to their mother and pointing at his car. He feared that they knew he had kidnapped the little girl and would call the police. He had to get back to his house as quickly as possible without drawing any attention or by driving too fast.

He heard the little girl laughing at something. He couldn't hear anyone else talking to her. Why was she laughing? Was she crazy? Did he make a mistake and pick up a weird one this time? He was having second thoughts about keeping her. Maybe he should just drop her off at the nearest corner store and just go on his way. He could look for another child. Parents nowadays left their children out in the yard to play all the time without checking on them very often. That is how he picked up the little boy.

The boy had been swinging on his swing set as he had walked up to the back of the house along the tree line. He had been wandering in the woods and noticed the little boy all by himself. He had called out softly to the little boy and asked him if he would like to play ball. The little boy no more than six years old evidently loved baseball and thought it was a good idea. The boy ran out to the woods to see the man who handed the boy a brand new baseball. The man had been watching this house and the child at play for about a week. He methodically planned the kidnapping this way. The man had watched the child playing with a baseball each time he had crept up to spy on him from the trees. The man had bought a new baseball just for this little boy.

The man was almost home now and the little girl still was talking up a storm. She was carrying on a full-fledged conversation with someone. Every so often she stopped talking as if she was listening to someone. Then she would laugh and respond as if she were answering someone.

The man parked the car outside of his house and got out to open the back door of the car to take the little girl out. Deanna looked surprised when the man pulled her out of the car and started to drag her to his house without a word. She looked up and said something to her imaginary friend asking for his help. The man stopped and looked at Deanna and asked her who she was talking to.

She started to cry because she didn't want to go with the man into the house and tried to pull her arm out of the man's grip. "I was talking to my daddy. I don't need to go with you now, I found my daddy. He told me that he is going to take me home."

"Oh no, you are not going anywhere but into my house. There is no one here but you and me. Your father is not here little girl. Don't you want to see something special that I have just for you?" The man pulled and tugged on the little girl as he tried to bring her closer to his front door. For whatever reason he wasn't making any headway though. The little girl didn't seem to be moving at all now. It was as if someone or something was holding her back. She continued to cry and speak in between sobs to someone above her. The man craned his head and looked up and all around him to see where she was looking.

CHAPTER SEVENTEEN

Priscilla had watched the Disney film with Robbie and he had fallen asleep somewhere in the middle. She had gently picked him up and put him to bed. Luckily she had already put him in his PJs so she didn't have to disturb him to do that now.

Priscilla turned off the TV and decided to call it an early night herself. She took a nice long bath and crawled into bed feeling content and sleepy. The minute her head hit the pillow she was fast asleep and soon dreaming.

Priscilla's thoughts were of her daughter and she could see Deanna being pulled away from her. She could hear her daughter's cries for help. Priscilla looked around in her dream but couldn't find Deanna. She saw a blinding white object coming toward her. It floated and blinked as it moved. She felt a kinship to this now familiar light.

The white object came closer and closer but it never touched her, but she felt calm and safe, not at all threatened. Priscilla tried to talk to the white object to ask it to help her daughter who was crying. Priscilla felt that the white object would take care of Deanna and that she shouldn't worry about her daughter. She felt a calm presence around the white object as it hovered over and around her. It was not a dream. It was really in her room. Something touched her face fleetingly like a butterfly and then flit away. Priscilla watched in awe once again as Parker appeared in front of her and flew away on a pair of large white wings into the bright white light.

The next morning Priscilla remembered her dream. She was worried about the fact that she heard Deanna's cries but the white object had calmed her fears and told Priscilla not to worry, it would take care of Deanna. *Would Parker as the guardian angel really take care of Deanna?* Should she call Sergeant Furelli? Should she tell someone about this in the morning?

Priscilla poured herself a cup of coffee as she prepared scrambled eggs and toast for her and Robbie. Robbie chatted animatedly from his booster seat as he ate his breakfast. Priscilla could only half listen to him as she sipped her coffee and picked at her eggs. Her mind kept going back to her dream last night and Deanna. She found herself reaching for the phone and dialing the police department number without thinking. The dispatcher came on the line saying, "Leah Mills Police Department. You are being recorded."

"This is Priscilla Wilfork and I need to speak with Sergeant Furelli."

"Yes, Mrs. Wilfork. He is out on a call right now but I will give him a message for you. Can I help you in any way? Is this an emergency?"

"Oh no, not really an emergency but it is important that I speak to him. You can give him my cell number since I will be leaving the house shortly to take my son to school." Priscilla rattled off her cell phone number and turned to clean up the table and get Robbie ready for preschool.

CHAPTER EIGHTEEN

"Gus, do you remember the little boy who was reported missing about six weeks ago?" Blake Furelli asked his partner as he started up the squad car to go on rounds.

It was turning out to be a beautiful sunny but crisp day in early fall. This time of year was always Blake's favorite. He looked forward to taking some time off to play catch with his son this weekend and maybe cook out for one last time before it got too cold. Matthew always loved hot dogs on the grill and he liked the way Blake toasted the hot dog rolls too. Blake found himself feeling very content and happy at the thought of a full weekend without work. But his mind returned to the present as he heard Gus answering his question.

"Yes, I remember the little boy, Peter something, wasn't it? The parents just called this morning before I came in. I had a message on my desk to call them back. I told the dispatcher, Janellen, that you were the responding officer but I would fill you in on whatever the parents wanted. I know you have a lot on your plate with this little girl who is missing. But if you would rather call them back, I can give you their number." Gus felt around in his pocket for the piece of paper with the phone number. He looked at it and handed it over to Blake saying, "Carter, that's their name."

"That is strange, Gus, that they called. I was just thinking of the case yesterday when I was leaving work. There is something very familiar between these two missing children's reports. Remind me to pull out the files on both of them when we get back after we make our rounds. We could look the files over after lunch time. Also, we need to pull Parker Wilfork's file and review that. Maybe we missed something that could connect to Deanna's disappearance. Oh, by the way, I promised you a sub or wrap or something. Ok? We can stop over at Ralph's Sandwich Shop," Blake grinned at his partner when he saw Gus' face light up at the thought of food.

"You know how to get to my heart through my stomach. I love you, Blake!"

"You are something else, Gus! I don't know where you put it – on the other hand, I can see where it ends up," Blake chuckled as he reached over and patted his partner's round belly.

Blake's face took on a serious expression as he asked, "Gus, do you remember anything particular about the little boy's disappearance?"

"No, there isn't anything that comes to mind, but my mind is not what it used to be!" Gus just shook his head, "I can't remember much these days unless it happened yesterday."

"Okay, old man, I understand. We will just have to review the files after you get some nourishment. How does that sound? Maybe food will bring back your memory."

"Blake, I know that you are really upset about these missing children. We will do all we can to find them. But you can't get emotionally or personally involved with the families. It will only cause you more grief in the end."

"Oh, and don't think I didn't catch the 'old man' comment from you. Enough of that from you, you young whippersnapper!" Gus first snarled at Blake but then smiled.

Blake felt a fondness for his partner who was more like a father to him than a partner. There were times when Blake felt he couldn't cut it as a police officer and then he would talk it over with Gus. Gus would somehow convince Blake that he was a wonderful officer and was doing a great job and that he was proud of Blake as a man and a fellow policeman.

This was one of the times that Blake wished he could stay unemotional or impersonal about these two missing child cases. Blake just couldn't distance himself. He had to find them or he wouldn't be able to look himself in the mirror again.

Blake had become very serious and intense staring out at the road ahead as he drove on their rounds. Chief of Police Angelo Sangeovese had told them to check out the Leah Mills Elementary School parking lot for any strange men waiting there for unsuspecting children. There had been a report of such a person there yesterday afternoon and again this morning. This report greatly disturbed Gus and Blake especially since the little girl was reported missing recently. It would be good if it was this easy to catch the culprit. Blake knew it wouldn't be that easy.

The man, reported being seen, could just be a parent waiting for his child and not the kidnapper they were looking for. But once in a while you could get lucky. Blake knew that Gus didn't feel very lucky today though. He had overslept this morning and then had a flat tire and arrived late for work. Blake had covered for Gus whenever he had come in late after he overslept due to a hangover or just forgot to turn on his alarm clock. Gus was becoming very forgetful lately.

Blake pulled up to the school and drove around the parking lot looking for anyone sitting in a car at this early morning hour. There was the usual amount of cars but no one sitting in any of them. Blake called into the dispatcher and told her that no one was in the parking lot of the elementary school. Janellen told Blake, "Chief Sangeovese requested that you go in and speak with Principal John Harden."

Blake responded, "Okay, will do," signed off, and got out of the car waiting an extra minute or two for his partner as he watched Gus gingerly pull himself up from his seat and catch up to him. Blake caught himself before saying something nasty to Gus about getting old. He knew that Gus didn't like to be called old; in fact he darn right hated it. Blake had already called him 'old man' once today. Just the same, the thought of how Gus would have reacted to this quip about being old made Blake smile which was noticed by his old but very observant partner.

As Gus walked alongside Blake he looked at his partner and smiled, knowing what brought on that smirk on his younger partner's face. Blake winked at Gus and couldn't help but chuckle. Blake had almost forgotten how very sharp Gus could be at times for an old man (in Blake's mind).

Blake and Gus both put their game faces on before entering the school. They had to ring a bell for security before entering. The schools had recently been equipped with locks and keycards for the staff. No one was allowed to enter without using a keycard or being rung through by one of the secretaries in the main office. There had been a few scares over the years about people being able to just walk into the school without being checked in by staff. It did not make for a very safe environment for the children or staff especially with the known violence all over the country of people going on killing sprees in government offices, schools and even movie houses. It could happen even in this quiet community of Leah Mills.

Principal John Harden met the officers as they entered the school. John introduced himself to Sergeant Furelli and Lieutenant Wholley as the policemen pulled out their identification badges. Principal Harden brought the policemen back to his office but before closing the door told his secretary to hold all calls or other interruptions until he was through meeting with the police.

John Harden motioned the policemen to two comfortable chairs in front of his desk as he took a seat behind his desk and looked up at Sergeant Furelli and Lieutenant Wholley. "Thank you, Officers, for getting here so quickly. I know you are busy with other issues but I greatly appreciate you coming."

"Mr. Harden, we are only doing our jobs. We take every report seriously too especially when it involves the safety of anyone, whether it is a child or an adult."

John Harden took a deep breath before continuing. His face went go gray and the wrinkles around his eyes more prominent as if what he had to tell them caused him to age. He nodded his thanks to the officers then began to explain why he had called the police station.

"There has been a car driving by the school as the children are going out for recess. Sometimes this car has stopped and watched the children at play. A few of the staff on duty outside reported this car to me on a couple of occasions. It was a green Honda Accord probably a 2008 or 2007 model. One of the staff was quick enough to copy down the license plate as it drove away. I wrote the plate number on this paper for you officers. I would appreciate anything you can do to catch this person. I feel that he may be a threat to our children. He may not have done anything at this point but I would feel a whole lot better knowing that you picked him up to speak with him."

"We will do all we can to find him. Thank you for the license plate number. This will definitely be a help. If you do see this man again, please call us right away. In the meantime we are going to run this plate and pay this man a visit. It was a pleasure to meet you, Mr. Harden. The next time we meet will hopefully be to deliver good news to you." John Harden thanked the officers again for their diligence as he offered his hand to them. Blake and Gus shook Mr. Harden's hand and left his office. Blake glanced at the paper Mr. Harden had given him with the plate number on it. He planned on calling the station to check out the plate as soon as they got back to their patrol car.

CHAPTER NINETEEN

"Hey, Janellen, it's Furelli. I have a plate I want you to check." Blake read off the plate and waited for the dispatcher to get back to him. In the meantime he pulled out his cell and called the Carters to see what they wanted to tell him.

"Hello Mrs. Carter, this is Sergeant Furelli from Leah Mills Police Department. I got a message that you wanted to talk to me. I am sorry we don't have any news for you about Peter yet."

"Oh, Sergeant Furelli, we have news for you. We are very relieved to report that our son, Peter, just came home. Well, he was found wandering around a playground nearby our house by one of our neighbors and was a little dirty but otherwise okay. He wasn't hurt or anything. We are going to take him to the pediatrician now and have him checked over thoroughly. I knew you would want to know right away. I can't thank you enough for your patience with us. I know I bothered you every day and made it difficult for you. But I...we are so happy that Peter came back to us." Mrs. Carter took a breath and sniffled and blew her nose.

"That is wonderful news. What is the doctor's address? I would like to meet you at the doctor's office to hear what the doctor has to say and then talk with Peter. He may have something important to tell us about his abductor. Thank you for calling me and telling me this good news. It is a relief to all of us to have him safely home."

"Okay, Sergeant Furelli." Mrs. Carter gave him the doctor's address and hung up.

Gus was picking his teeth with a toothpick but closely watching his fellow officer. He waited as Blake hung up the phone and looked at him before asking what had just happened.

"What happened?" Gus queried.

"Well, you probably figured out what that was all about. It seems Peter Carter is now safe and well at home. His parents reported that he was picked up on the playground near their home by a neighbor and brought home to them. He appeared to be in good health outside of being a little dirty. They are taking him now to their pediatrician to have him checked over and we are meeting them at the doctor's office to talk to Peter after his exam. The doctor may be able to tell us if he was injured in any way."

"Wow, that is a strange one. Where the hell was he all that time and how did he end up at the playground? We have been combing the streets for six weeks now looking for him and he just strolls home on his own?" Gus expressed his surprise as Blake drove to meet the Carters.

"My questions exactly, Gus. I want to see this boy and talk to him. He may be able to tell us something. Why was he let go by the abductor? Something doesn't add up here. If this person is a pedophile, they don't act that way. They don't steal children and then let them go. Maybe Peter escaped on his own and ran away. We won't know until we talk to Peter. Hopefully he will remember and give us a good description of the man who took him. He could be in state of shock and unstable right now. But we need to try. Whatever he can tell us, may bring us closer to finding Deanna."

Blake was relieved to have the boy back home but something was bothering him about this abduction and he couldn't put his finger on it. He wouldn't rest until he did. It brought his mind back to Priscilla and her daughter. There may be hope for Deanna to return unharmed. He could only pray that was the case.

Blake was nearly at the doctor's office when he received a call from dispatch about the plate.

"Hi Janellen. What ya got for me?"

"Well, Sergeant It seemed that the plate has been stolen from a car left in a parking lot outside the Mill

Restaurant in town last week. I looked up the owner and he had reported it stolen. Two officers are heading over there to check out the video tapes from the parking lot. I will call you back with the results, ASAP. Sorry Sergeant I don't have more for you. I put out an APB on the Honda."

"Thanks Janellen. Let me know if anything turns up, okay?"

"Sure thing, Sergeant! Oh, before I go I also have a message for you from Mrs. Wilfork. She wants you to call her. She didn't say what it was about only that it wasn't an emergency."

"Okay, thanks Janellen. I will call her as soon as I can."

"This didn't lead us anywhere," Blake stated. "But we may see something on the video tape from the parking lot of the restaurant. Janellen will call us back after two of our guys checked it out." He looked at Gus and his partner just shook his head.

"Yeah, it sounded too easy to have been given a license plate on this guy. It never happens like that in real life, only in the movies." Gus looked out the window and sighed.

"The important thing is we do not give up on this little girl. We have to find her. Umm, listen Gus, can you follow up and call Principal Harden about the plate. You know what else to do with surveillance, partner. I need to call Priscilla and follow up there after we meet with Peter and his parents."

"Yeah, I bet you do, Blake." Gus chuckled as he made a few notes in his notebook for the principal. Under his breath Gus added, *I bet you do, Blake. Just don't get hurt.*

"Did you say something, Partner?"

"Huh, no, just talking to myself, Blake," Gus retorted.

"Listen Gus, don't worry about me, okay? The person you should be worrying about is this little girl."

"Okay, I agree. But I can still worry about you at the same time. We will find her, Blake. I will do all I can to help, I promise."

"Thanks, Gus. I appreciate your help. You know that. We are partners and we will do this together. Okay?"

"Yep, you got it, Blake!"

The rest of the way they were both quiet as Blake arrived at the doctor's office to meet the Carters and speak with little Peter. As Blake and Gus entered the doctor's office they went over to the Carters who were sitting there looking anxious as Peter sat on his mother's lap with his head on her shoulder.

After waiting for another ten minutes Dr. DeCesare came out to meet the Carters and bring Peter back to an examining room. Sergeant Furelli and Lieutenant Wholley introduced themselves and asked, "Dr. DeCesare we need to speak with you after your examination of Peter Carter. As Mr. & Mrs. Carter reported to you Peter was kidnapped and recently returned home. We are following up on the case."

The doctor nodded and responded, "I see. Please follow me and wait in this adjacent examination room and I will come back there after examining Peter to speak with you."

"Thank you, Doctor." Blake and Gus made themselves comfortable in the room and called into the station to report where they were and that they may be there for at least another hour and a half.

Gus twiddled his thumbs and looked at Blake who was in somewhat of a stupor. "Hey Blake, what are you thinking about? Do you think the doctor will find evidence of foul play on Peter?"

Blake looked up at Gus and sighed, "I don't know Gus? I just don't know. I am hoping for Peter's sake that he does not find anything like that. Peter does look like he is still in shock over the whole thing. Poor kid, he is only six. I swear, Gus, we have got to get this guy soon."

"I know, Blake. We will, Buddy, we will!"

Forty-five minutes went by when the door to the room they were in opened and in walked Dr. DeCesare looking puzzled but composed.

Blake spoke before the doctor could, anxious to learn the doctor's findings, "Hi Doctor. What did you find?"

Dr. DeCesare looked into Blake's blue eyes and slowly responded in a calm voice, "I didn't find any signs of injury to the boy. Peter was nervous but he was not harmed in any way, if you know what I mean, Officers. I think you need to speak with Peter yourself and he will tell you what transpired."

"Thank you, Doctor. We appreciate you taking the time to fill us in. Can we use this room to speak with the Carters now?" Blake asked.

"Yes, certainly. I will tell my nurse to keep this room opened for you for as long as you need it." Dr. DeCesare shook Sergeant Furelli and Lieutenant

Wholley's hands and took his leave. On his way out the doctor held the door open for Mr. & Mrs. Carter and Peter to enter.

Mrs. Carter held onto Peter's hand protectively as she led him into the room to meet with the officers. Peter did not look up at them until Sergeant Furelli addressed him.

"Hello, Peter. I am Sergeant Furelli and this is Lieutenant Wholley. We are officers in the Leah Mills Police Department. We heard about you returning home recently. How are you doing, Peter?" Blake smiled at Peter to try to put him at ease.

Mrs. Carter patted her son on the back and whispered in his ear to answer the officer.

"I'm good, Mr. Officer." Peter responded with his head down.

"Peter, can you tell me where you were all this time? Do you know the person's name who took you?"

Peter looked up for the first time to meet Sergeant Furelli's eyes and responded, "No, I was far from home. I don't know where the house was and I don't know who the man was either. I know the boy's name who lived there. His name was Jeremy. We played together but I wanted to come home. I didn't like being there. I missed my Mommy." Peter began to cry and reach for his mother who took him into her arms and held onto him as she looked at Sergeant Furelli with a stern warning.

Sergeant Furelli waved her warning aside and continued with his questioning, "Peter, we need to know if this man hurt you in any way."

Mrs. Carter shook her head at Sergeant Furelli and was on the verge of tears at this questioning. "Sergeant Furelli, what are you trying to do to my son? You already know that he is fine by what Dr. DeCesare said. Why are you asking Peter this question? The doctor told us that Peter only needs to be home and feel safe once again with us."

"I want to hear your son tell me what happened at this house. There may be something he can tell us. We have a little girl missing now and she may have been taken by the same man."

"Oh, I am sorry about this little girl but I have to think about my son's wellbeing."

"If you do not let him answer these questions here then you will have to come down to the station."

Mrs. Carter sighed and said, "I...okay, Sergeant."

"Now, I have a few more questions for Peter, Mrs. Carter. Peter, what color was the house you were taken to? Do you remember if it was a big house or a small house with only a few rooms?"

Peter scrunched up his face as he thought about what the officer asked him, "I think it was blue. I only stayed in the boy's bedroom with him. I didn't see any other rooms."

"Did the man feed you and take care of you while you were there?"

"Yes, I ate mac and cheese and hotdogs and broccoli which I don't like. Yuck!" Peter was relaxing more with each answer he gave.

Blake continued as he was watched closely by Mrs. Carter who still looked wary of the questioning. "Now Peter, can you tell me what this man looks like? What color is his hair? Is he short or tall?"

Blake knew that Peter would think everyone is tall to him since he was just a little boy but he felt that anything Peter could tell him would be helpful.

Peter shook his head, "I don't remember what he looked like. I was too scared and didn't want to look at him. He left me in the room with Jeremy every day and locked the door. I didn't like that."

"Okay, Peter. That's all right. What can you tell me about the man? Just take your time and think about it."

"He talked softly to me and to Jeremy. He never raised his voice like my Daddy does sometimes." Peter looked at his father who was sitting quietly observing the interchange. Mr. Carter smiled and nodded to Peter saying, "Sometimes I do, Peter, for that I am sorry, son."

"That's good, Peter. Anything else you can remember?" Blake responded continuing the exchange.

"He kissed Jeremy a lot and put him on the potty all the time and gave him a bath every night. He told me to wash myself but he did fill the tub for me too and I got in by myself and washed all up. Mommy helps me do that at home. I missed you, Mommy," Peter turned to his mother after this statement and snuggled in her arms.

"How did you get away from the man, Peter? Did he just let you go?"

"No, I opened up the window and jumped down and ran away. I didn't know the way to go home but kept walking until I got to the park. I knew it was close to my house. Then I saw my friend's mother and she brought me home."

"Well, you are a smart boy to do that, Peter. Now you are home safe. I guess that is enough for now, Peter. Maybe you can tell me more later. If you remember anything please tell your mommy and she will call me so we can talk again, okay?" Blake patted Peter on the head and shook Mr. Carter's hand and waved to Mrs. Carter over Peter's head. She just smiled wanly at him and nodded.

Peter suddenly picked up his head off his mother's shoulder and responded, "Brown."

"What did you say, Peter?" his mother asked.

"I think the man's hair was brown, Mommy," Mrs. Carter looked at Sergeant Furelli.

"Okay, Peter. That is very helpful. Thank you for remembering," Blake smiled relieved that he had at least something to go on.

"Thank you, Mr. & Mrs. Carter. I will keep in touch with you. If Peter remembers anything else at all, please call me immediately. Bye, Peter. Nice talking to you." Blake smiled warmly at Peter as he headed out of the room with Gus in tow.

Blake needed time to absorb the news about Peter Carter's strange reappearance and what little the boy could tell him about his abductor. Blake knew he needed to work on his next strategy to find Deanna. He would need all the help he could get. A little prayer wouldn't hurt either, he thought.

CHAPTER TWENTY

JemsWorld store

Priscilla drove back home after dropping Robbie off at school. She didn't stay to work but instead made an excuse that she needed to get some important things done. Priscilla felt like she needed to look into the store to find out what was going on there. It was something to do to keep her mind active and keep her sane with Deanna missing. She felt so helpless that she couldn't do anything to find Deanna on her own. Maybe she could work at the store and feel close to Parker in some way. She didn't know why she hadn't thought of this sooner. Stress can do strange things to people and she definitely had more than her share of stress.

She called ahead to the two partners and told them that she would be stopping by to check in on things. Redmond Somers seemed a little nervous about her going to the store but did not say anything. His tone of voice told her. However, when she talked to Mark Ford he came right out with, "Listen Priscilla, there is no need for you to go to the store. Did you think we couldn't deal with the day-to-day handling of things?"

"Oh no, I did not want to insinuate any such thing, Mark. I am sorry you feel that way. I haven't been at the store very often since Parker's disappearance and wanted to see how things were going. I appreciate that you have been depositing money into my account regularly. It has been a godsend to me and the children. I think the customers should see me visible from time to time to allay their fears of the store closing with Parker missing. Don't you think? I know I should have come in sooner, but I have had a difficult time dealing with everything."

"Well okay, if you would like me to meet you there I can show you around and introduce you to the new people."

"What new people, Mark? Did you hire anyone else since Parker...?" Priscilla's tone changed from calm to anxious.

"Well, the new boss sent some people over to the store to do the shipping and handling of all products. We no longer deal with that and put all our efforts into the daily handling of the store and ordering. Didn't you know that? I thought the new boss had called you. He told us that he would take care of informing you and that we shouldn't concern ourselves about getting involved."

"What are you talking about, Mark? What new boss? Did you sell the store out from under me? How could you do that? Parker owns 51%. You couldn't possibly do that without his or my signature and I have no plans to do any such thing! Why wouldn't you tell me about this? Does Atty. Frederickson know about this? The exchange would have to go through him," Priscilla's voice was rising and so was her temper.

"Wait just a minute, Priscilla. We didn't do any such thing. We never met the man or know his name. He sent a paper to us with Parker's signature on it signing over the 51% of the store to him. Evidently Parker did this before he disappeared. I don't know anything more about this. The guy warned us not to get involved. I told you that already. He wanted to take care of this himself. He told us that he would fire us if we got in his way or told you anything." Mark was anxious now and didn't know what else to say.

"When did this happen, Mark? Wait…did you say paper with Parker's signature?" Priscilla was holding her breath as she waited for his answer.

"Well, I guess it was over a year ago when the man contacted us. He said he was going to talk to you soon and get things rolling. His men showed up shortly after that. Oh, about the paper with his signature, it was shown to us by one of the new men but he took it back. We don't have it now, sorry."

"That is just great! You've got to be kidding? Over a year ago you say? What is going on here, Mark?

Never mind. I am going to contact my lawyer. Steven should have called me. I plan to get to the bottom of this. I will talk to both of you later."

Priscilla abruptly hung up the phone not waiting to hear any more from the partner. Come to think of it, she hadn't heard from her attorney in over a year. She thought about that now but hadn't given it any concern since he promised to contact her with any new developments. Then with Deanna missing Priscilla couldn't even think straight about why he hadn't called her. She had told Steven not to bring up Parker's will until she was ready. She hoped against hope that Parker would return but she knew otherwise. He wasn't ever coming back. Her dreams had told her that. She just had to accept his death but needed to know why and how.

Priscilla knew she had not spoken to either partner in almost two years thinking that they were handling everything. As long as the money kept coming into her account she didn't worry about it or even think about the store. She had noticed the amount of money had tripled but she figured business was good and didn't question it. She should have questioned this but she had needed all the help she could get to pay the bills. It was a reminder that Parker was gone and she couldn't go into the store. She had only gone into the store on a few occasions and went out of her way to get home deliveries most weeks.

Now she was feeling frightened about this matter. There were a myriad of questions going around in her head.

What did it mean? Did she no longer own the store? Why did the new owner not pay her for Parker's share? Is that why she was still receiving weekly payments… to keep her quiet? Who was this partner that Parker had given up the store to? Why would Parker do that without telling her first? And, why didn't her lawyer call her about this change? Did Steven even know about it?

Priscilla grabbed her cell and scrolled to Steven's number to hear what he had to say about this. She nervously tapped her foot as she waited for her call to go through to voicemail. She left him an irate message and hung up. "Steven call me immediately about the store. You have some explaining to do!"

Priscilla paced the kitchen floor and looked around for something to clean. She always cleaned when she was nervous or upset. She grabbed some disinfectant spray and cleaned the counters, sink and stove putting more than enough effort into already cleaned areas.

Next she went into the bathrooms and scrubbed them and sprayed the mirrors until they glistened. Normally when she cleaned she put on some music to make cleaning more fun. She wasn't into making these tasks fun but wanted to get rid of her anger. She knew she had to calm down before she spoke to Steven. There had to be a perfectly good explanation. But she couldn't fathom one.

Her cell rang suddenly and she nearly dropped the spray into the toilet trying to juggle and get to her cell phone in her back pocket. She connected to the call and heard a woman's voice.

"Hello, Mrs. Wilfork? This is Attorney Steven Frederickson's secretary/paralegal. How can I help you? Counselor Frederickson is unavailable and is out of state at this time."

"I need to speak with him immediately. This is extremely important."

"Well, Counselor Frederickson has given me permission to review all his cases since he is not scheduled to come back to the office any time soon. In fact, I do not know when he will return. Now, please let me help you, Mrs. Wilfork. By your message you sounded very upset."

"Yes, you bet I am upset. Are you aware that my husband's store was sold out from under me over a year ago? Did Steven know about this and why didn't he tell me?" Priscilla felt anger building up inside her once again.

"Let me pull your file, Mrs. Wilfork, then we can talk more. All right? Just a moment please." The secretary put Priscilla on hold while she looked for the file.

"Ah yes, I see. I found some notes I had made. Can't seem to find the file though. Yes, it seems that it was sold by your husband to a large construction company out in Los Angeles, California. The company the store was sold to plans to open up another JemsWorld store out there in a super mall."

"Counselor Frederickson took care of this himself and went out to California to complete the transaction. I thought he had informed you of this. He did make sure that you continued to receive your payments monthly indefinitely from the store to help you and the children out. The new company agreed to that. Are you all right, Mrs. Wilfork?"

"I am sorry you did not know about this. Steven went out to California and decided to extend his time there to work with the new company. He left word with the other lawyers that they would take over all his clients. I wish I could help you in some way but I don't know if I will have this job for much longer. I am a legal secretary with experience as a paralegal and can't do anything more than assist clients. I can't solve their problems in court. There are other lawyers in our building that you could call.

I may call them myself to find out what I am going to do about closing this office. Counselor Frederickson paid me over a years' wages to stay on but that time is about up and I have to leave."

"I am sorry for you too, umm… what is your name?"

"My name is Sally. I apologize for any problems this has caused you, Mrs. Wilfork. Is there anything else I can do for you?"

"No Sally, I guess there isn't. I am not angry with you but I am with Steven. If you do hear back from him please let me know. But for now, can you give me the other lawyers' numbers so I can call them? Maybe one of them can help me figure this out."

"Oh, of course. Just a moment and I will get them for you."

Reading off the numbers Sally said, "I hope one of them can help you, Mrs. Wilfork."

"Yes, so do I. And, it is Priscilla, Sally. Thank you for your help. Maybe you should see if you can get a job with these other lawyers in your building."

"I was thinking the same thing, Priscilla. Thank you too. Take care and I hope it all turns out the way you want. I will keep looking for the file and if you need me to fax it to the lawyers please call me."

"Thank you, Sally, I will. Goodbye," Priscilla put down the phone and noticed her hands were shaking. She couldn't believe what was happening.

She tried to calm herself down but found that all she could do was cry out her frustrations. She thought over her life these two years since Parker's disappearance. It was hard enough to lose him and now Deanna was still missing and no word about her whereabouts. Her crazy dreams about Parker as an angel came to mind. *Could the angel help her find Deanna? How was this even possible?*

More questions to be answered: *What was she going to do? How was she going to survive without the proceeds from the store if the money suddenly stopped coming to her? Why didn't Steven or the other partners call her? Why did they keep her in the dark? Who was this new partner? Did he know where Parker disappeared to? Was he responsible for Parker's disappearance?*

Priscilla looked at the list of phone numbers in her hand and placed a call to the first one. She had to get things rolling and save her family and the store.

The secretary answered on the second ring and Priscilla told her the problem. She was given an appointment for the next morning when Robbie was in school. Priscilla didn't want to bring him with her in case she got upset.

Her home phone started to ring as she had finished the call on her cell. Priscilla hoped this was some good news about Deanna. Maybe, dear God, she was found.

"Priscilla, this is Sergeant Blake Furelli. Are you okay?"

"Yes, I am as best as can be expected. Do you have any news about Deanna?"

"No, not about Deanna."

"I was hoping you did have some good news for me. I just received some bad news today about my husband's store."

"Oh what's happened? Do you want to talk about it? I can come over right now. That is why I was calling. I had some new developments in the case and wanted to share them with you."

"What, did you find Deanna?" Priscilla asked on the verge of crying.

"No, but some news about another child being found."

"Oh dear God! That is good news. But what about Deanna?"

"We are hopeful that we will find her. I will be over in a few minutes. We'll talk more then. Okay?"

"Yeah, okay," Priscilla sighed and shivered at the same time. She was feeling overwhelmed with her losses. She didn't want to think negatively. She knew losing the store was not the end of the world but if she lost Deanna…it would be!

***

Sally looked through the files for the Wilfork file in vain. She tried the old file cabinet and then again the new one thinking maybe Steven or she had filed it incorrectly. It was not there.

CHAPTER TWENTY-ONE

Blake didn't like the sound of Priscilla's voice when he called. She may be on the verge of a nervous breakdown if he couldn't find Deanna soon, he thought. It has only been a little over a week since she disappeared but seemed like much longer. He had to move quicker to find Deanna. The whole precinct had been out combing the area every day with no sign of her.

As Blake pulled up outside Priscilla's house he saw her looking out the window at him. He got out of the squad car and hurried up the walk to the front door. He only wished he could give Priscilla something positive about finding Deanna. But having Peter Carter back was comforting and showed promise that maybe Deanna would come home too that way.

***

Priscilla watched Blake as he walked up to her door. He looked like the world was resting on his shoulders. She knew she was leaning heavily on him too much lately. But she didn't know where else to turn. He was her only hope to find Deanna. Besides, she found his company comforting and enjoyed seeing him. She saw something in his eyes that he may feel the same about her.

***

Priscilla opened the door and welcomed Blake in and told him to get comfortable in the living room. She excused herself to make some coffee and pulled some of her cake out of the freezer to warm up. Blake clearly enjoyed it last time. She also needed to keep busy because she still had the shakes from the present news. Priscilla didn't want Blake to think of her as an incompetent woman who cried all the time. She straightened her shoulders and took the laden tray into the living room.

Blake watched Priscilla come toward him with the tray of coffees and cake. She looked like she was trying to keep herself together but her furrowed brow showed her deep anxiety over yet another loss in her life.

"Priscilla, please sit down and tell me what has upset you."

She sat down and sighed as she began to unburden herself to Blake. He didn't interrupt and listened carefully to her surprising news. In the back of his mind he was already planning to pay a visit to this new owner in Los Angeles, California soon.

"Okay, now you have not received compensation for this sale, have you, Priscilla?"

"Well, not officially, but the payments that the partners are depositing in my checking account have tripled lately without any explanation. I thought that the store was doing well and didn't give it much thought. I was grateful for the money to pay the bills. I don't make much at the school as an aide and by selling my crafts. I haven't visited the store much since Parker's disappearance. It's been too painful for me. But today I decided to go. I called the partners first to give them a heads-up."

"I understand, Priscilla. Now, you mentioned that your lawyer disappeared after Parker, well over a year ago? He never contacted you about the sale and suddenly you are receiving more money in your account from the store. It sounds like the new boss is slowly giving you the money but in a strange way. I need to have a talk with this new boss. Do you know his name?"

"No, that is what is even stranger. No one seems to know his name. Parker's partners said they saw a paper with Parker's signature on it signing over the store to the new owner. But they claim they do not have the paper now. The man's name must be on the documents he signed with Parker though. I need to get a copy of the document. My lawyer's secretary is going to fax a copy to my new lawyer when I tell her where to send it. I will ask her to send me a copy too, okay? It seems that my lawyer, Steven

Frederickson, was contacted by the man and went out to California to seal the deal. Steven hasn't returned since. Looks like he must be doing better out there than here. But he never even told me about this. I don't understand why."

"That would be a good idea to get a copy. Let me know when you receive it. I need to speak with the chief and get permission to follow up on this. It does seem strange that your lawyer now is missing. Going there may lead to some clues about what happened to Parker. Maybe I will be able to contact your lawyer too."

"I have a feeling that Deanna's disappearance could be connected to Parker's, Sergeant."

"Please call me Blake. I don't know about that but let's see what I can find out when I get out there. Lieutenant Wholley will hold the fort for me here and follow up on finding Deanna. Oh, I nearly forgot, Priscilla. I need to fill you in on what happened about the lost boy that was found."

"Yes, oh yes, you did mention you were going to tell me about him. What happened to him? When did he go missing?"

Blake relayed the message from Mrs. Carter about Peter being found in the playground near her house and being missing for six weeks.

He continued on, "Gus and I then met with Peter's doctor in his office after his examination of Peter. The doctor told us that Peter was not harmed physically but mentally he is withdrawn and anxious. He is only six years old after all and this has been a traumatic experience. Why this man kidnapped him is a mystery to me. Peter did not give us too much information about the man except that he had brown hair and was good to his son, Jeremy, and him. The man fed them and made sure that Peter took baths at night all by himself. Peter stressed that part without my asking. This man did not kidnap Peter because he was a pedophile but for another reason, but what, I don't know."

"Oh thank God Peter is okay and unharmed. My heart goes out to his poor parents who had to wait six weeks to get him back. Didn't Peter give you a description of his kidnapper or where he was taken? He must know something. I know he is too young...I'm sorry. I feel as if I am dying just from nine days with Deanna gone. It may take him awhile to get over this. I only hope that Deanna is unharmed too and comes home soon like Peter did. I don't want to think that she ...," Priscilla stopped as she found words would not come.

Blake could see that Priscilla must be imagining the worst especially after what he had said about Peter being unharmed. He heard her take a deep breath and whisper a silent prayer for Deanna's guardian angel to watch over her.

"It's okay. I was disappointed too that Peter couldn't give me more information about the man but, like you say, he is very young. Priscilla, we will find Deanna and bring her home. I will do whatever I have to do to get her back. Now what you need to do is concentrate on Robbie and yourself and stay strong for when Deanna comes home. She will need you."

"Thank you, Blake, I don't know what I would do without you. I feel as if I would fall apart if not for your confidence and strength."

"Priscilla, you don't give yourself much credit here. You are stronger than you realize. You are handling everything on your own. I am only doing my part and that is to find Deanna and make sure the person who took her is punished."

Blake found he was sharing a lot more than he probably should have with Priscilla but couldn't help himself. He wanted to give her more hope that Deanna would be found. The idea that someone had taken Deanna was tearing him up too. He vowed he would do whatever he could to find her. But for now, he planned to travel to California to find out what went wrong there for Parker. Of course, he had to first convince his chief that this trip was necessary after two years.

Blake sat a little longer with Priscilla to calm her down and discussed the store and when it was started and odds and ends about each other's lives. Blake knew he had to go or would be answering to his chief why he was so late getting back to the station. He excused himself and pocketed another slice of cake for later after Priscilla offered to wrap it up for him. He looked into her blue eyes and saw something there that he hadn't seen since his wife, hope for a new future for both of them.

Blake took Priscilla's hand and held it a little too long before squeezing it. He felt a squeeze back from her and both smiled while looking deep into each other's blue eyes before breaking contact.

"Priscilla, I need to go now but I will get back to you as soon as I can about my trip as long as Chief gives me the okay. In the meantime I will follow up on some leads. This abductor could be one and the same that has taken Deanna."

"Oh Blake! I pray to God that you find out something. Thank you for all you are doing to help me. I feel like I am at the end of my rope and it is getting pretty frayed."

"I know, Priscilla. I don't know how you are holding up but believe me, I will be here for you whenever you need me. All you have to do is call. Here is my cell and home phone numbers in case you can't reach me at work," Blake handed his card with his personal numbers jotted on the back. He knew now he had crossed the line from a business relationship to a personal one. He had never done this before. He only hoped he could come through for Priscilla and find her daughter and do his job professionally at the same time.

Priscilla looked at Blake and ran into his arms and held on tightly. She needed to feel his strength, hoping it would transfer to her, making her stronger in spirit. She did not know what was going to happen but she knew that Blake would be there for her.

Blake hugged her back and then let her go. They locked gazes that spoke of more than words as he smiled and turned toward the door. Words did not come to him because he felt overwhelmed at her display of affection.

Priscilla walked Blake to the door and waved as he got into his squad car. Blake waved back and pulled away with his mind whirling with his own unanswered questions about them and how he was going to solve Priscilla's problems. He knew she was depending upon him. He only hoped he would not disappoint her.

CHAPTER TWENTY-TWO

Deanna

Priscilla looked at her watch and realized it was almost time to pick up Robbie. She grabbed her pocketbook, phone, and keys and ran out to her car. She didn't want to be late. Robbie would be very upset and think she may have forgotten him. That she could never do. She loved him so fiercely and couldn't take losing him too.

Robbie was sitting at his desk as Priscilla came into his room to pick him up. He looked up at her with his beautiful smile and jumped up, ran to her and gave her his usual big hug.

Priscilla felt tears of joy filling her eyes. She didn't want to cry here in front of other people. She took Robbie's hand and brought him out to the car and drove home. She only hoped he wouldn't ask about Deanna again. She had been gone over a week now and Priscilla didn't know how long she could keep telling Robbie that Deanna was at a friend's house. She had never been away from home before even for one night.

***

Deanna couldn't see her father anymore. He had suddenly disappeared but not before telling her he would be back to get her.

The man pulled Deanna along into the house and closed the door and locked it. He dragged her to another room which was also locked and using the set of keys hanging from his belt opened the door. Inside she saw a little boy sitting on the bed coloring in a book. The boy looked up at her and yelled, "Daddy, you are home. I missed you. The other boy left me. He climbed out the window. I didn't want to go with him. Is he coming back again?" Jeremy ran over to hug his father.

The man just nodded at Jeremy and smiled. "It's okay Jeremy. I know the boy left. Don't worry about him. He went away and will not be coming back."

Jeremy soon forgot about the boy once he noticed the girl standing there looking at him.

"Who is this girl, Daddy? She's pretty!" The boy looked curiously at Deanna and touched her long blond hair and the blue butterfly clip.

"This is your new sister, Ashley. Say 'hi' to Ashley."

Jeremy smiled shyly at Deanna, "Hi Ashley. I like your hair."

Directing his attention toward Deanna, "Ashley, say 'hi' to your brother, Jeremy."

"No, he is not my brother. I have a brother and his name is Robbie. I want to go home. I miss my mother and brother. My father will be coming back to get me. He promised," Deanna started crying and rocking herself in place. The man couldn't budge Deanna as he tried to move her closer to Jeremy.

"Listen Ashley, I will bring you some clothes, books and toys so you can feel at home here with Jeremy. I need you to watch over him and feed him. I don't have anyone else to take care of him. I promise it will only be for a little while until I get some help. Then I will let you go." The man rubbed his forehead and wrung his hands as he watched for any reaction from Deanna.

"No, I want to go home now. My name is not Ashley. Please let me go home. I want my mother!" Deanna was now crying louder and stamping her feet to get the man's attention.

Jeremy went over to Deanna, "Please don't cry. I will be your friend. Please be my friend too. I am all alone and have no one to play with since the other boy left."

Deanna stopped crying and looked at Jeremy and asked, "What other boy?"

Before Jeremy could answer his father stepped in and picked him up and brought him to the bathroom to put him on the potty. He knew that Jeremy was getting better about going if reminded. He had put a pullup on him just in case he didn't make the bathroom in time.

His son was proud when he went on his own and wanted to show his new sister how big he was. After all he was almost four now. Jeremy had Down Syndrome. He was amazing in his resilience to bounce back after his mother's death last month. It may be because he did not understand where she went and thought she would come back one day.

Jeremy was always going to be a little boy mentally and his father knew he could not deal with taking care of him on his own. His son was upset when the other boy ran away reason why he had to find another child to look after Jeremy. He had tried to leave him alone and come home often from work to check on him at first. But once he got Jeremy to sleep he would slip out of the house and go to work again. The man knew he couldn't keep doing that or he would lose his job if his boss found out.

He had seen Deanna at MacIntosh's stand after picking up some apples and vegetables for Jeremy.

He promised his son to find him another brother or sister to keep him company and take care of him. He thought finding a girl this time would work out better like a little mother.

After Jeremy finished in the bathroom his father locked the door to the children's room and went out to the kitchen to prepare dinner for them. Before leaving the room he told the children, "Now why don't you two get acquainted while I make you some dinner? I will be back soon. I bought you some apples, Jeremy, your favorite kind, honey crisp. They are really sweet and delicious. You and Ashley can have one after dinner."

The man worked nights at JemsWorld store as a custodian/maintenance man for almost four years now. He wasn't making enough, however, to hire a full-time nanny/housekeeper for his son but hoped to save up enough money to have someone come in every day to feed and bathe Jeremy. The only thing he was afraid of was losing his son. He had lost his wife two months ago to ovarian cancer.

He really was not a bad person but did not think about how his actions had affected Deanna's family. He did not know where to turn for help. He had planned to talk to his boss at work to see if he could get a raise to help him along but he hadn't seen the boss in two years and there were rumors that he had disappeared and was not coming back. He never saw the other partners in the store nor did he know them well enough to ask them for help.

The man finished the children's dinner of mac and cheese and broccoli which was Jeremy's favorite – little trees which he dipped into the mac and cheese sauce. He was careful that Jeremy got enough vegetables and always included some in all meals. He fed his son before he went to work and made sure that he was comfortable telling Jeremy that he would be home soon. After dinner he would give Jeremy a bath and let him play on his bed with his toys until he got sleepy. Before going out the door he would check on his son and see him sleeping with his toys all around him on the bed. He would tuck him in and remove all the toys and lock the bedroom door before leaving for work. He did not want Jeremy to wander around the house and get into something in the kitchen and hurt himself in some way.

***

Deanna kept close watch over the man as he came in and out of the bedroom with their food and again to bath Jeremy and put him to bed. She went to the bathroom after Jeremy was done and cleaned up as she cried softly. She felt lost and couldn't see how she was going to get home. She didn't even know where she was. *If she ran away how would she know how to get home? Who would help her? Her father told her he would be back to get her. But when was he going to come? How was he going to get into the house? It was locked.*

Deanna got ready for bed and couldn't sleep at first tossing and turning in the twin bed next to Jeremy. She finally fell asleep but dreamt that she was sitting up in bed. She looked around at her surroundings and remembered she was not at home. A light appeared by the window and slowly moved toward her. She reached out to try to touch it but only felt its warmth. She strained to look at it more closely and jumped back when she was saw her father's face in the light. He was there with his giant angel wings and talking to her in her mind.

"Deanna, please don't be afraid. I am here close by even if you don't see me."

"Daddy, what happened to you? Why didn't you come home?" Deanna asked in a frightened voice.

"I am in a better place now, sweet one. You need not worry about me. I will keep watch over you. Sleep now, soon you will be safely back home," the angel responded.

After almost two weeks of taking care of Jeremy, Deanna, now known as Ashley to Jeremy, had become like a big sister to him. She read and bathed and dressed him and helped him go to the potty. He was almost fully potty trained now. The man had not been unkind to her, in fact, he had been very nice picking up some used clothes and books and some girl's toys for her. She did not want to stay here forever though. She missed her mother and brother and wanted to go home. Deanna wondered how her mother was doing and what she was doing to find her.

The guardian angel appeared each night in Deanna's dreams to comfort, assure and encourage her not to give up hope. He told her to look around for something to open the lock so she could escape.

Deanna decided that she would have to try to escape as her father, the angel, had suggested. After all, if the other boy escaped so could she. Jeremy had said the boy escaped out the window. But after looking out the window Deanna noticed that there were bars on the windows in the room making it difficult to get through. The man must have put them on after the boy had escaped, she surmised.

Deanna was an intelligent young girl and her parents always told her she could do anything she put her mind to on her own. Now was the time to do that, she thought.

Deanna looked around the room for something to use to work on the lock of the door as the angel in her dream instructed. If she could get out of this bedroom she could make enough noise and get help from neighbors or someone passing by.

Deanna kept Jeremy busy with his trucks and Duplo blocks so she could work on the lock with a spring she had found mixed in with Jeremy's toys. The angel watched as Deanna discovered the spring he had placed amongst the toys.

CHAPTER TWENTY-THREE

Missing Files

Blake couldn't believe that the chief had approved his trip to California to follow up on the Wilfork case. It took a little convincing on Blake's part but Chief finally approved him for three days out there. If Blake did not find out anything of value he was to report back immediately to him.

Chief warned, "Blake stay under the radar and don't make waves for you are out of your jurisdiction there. Whatever you do will be on me. I already discussed this case with the Los Angeles Police Department Chief and they closed the case after their investigation. They agreed to let us check out a few things as long as you stay out of trouble."

"Right, Chief. I understand. Maybe I will be lucky and find something that they did not. Thank you again."

Now all Blake had to do was call Priscilla and tell her that he would be going tomorrow morning and see her in three days, hopefully with good news. He wasn't expecting it to be good news but he was hoping that he could find out something about where Parker had disappeared too. He had to have left something behind or someone had seen him.

People don't just disappear off the face of the earth that easily without someone seeing them. Look what happened to Whitey Bulger, murderer/mobster in the USA. He was finally found. Well, Parker is hardly comparable to Bulger but he surely is being elusive like Whitey was.

***

Priscilla was pacing back and forth trying to put all the facts together and come up with something plausible. First, Parker went missing, then their lawyer, and finally Deanna. Were these disappearances all connected and why? She called Sally, her former lawyer's secretary, to give her the date and name of the lawyer she was going to see about the business. She waited for Sally to answer the phone as all these things were going around again in her head.

"Atty. Frederickson's office, Sally speaking. How may I help you?"

"Oh, Sally, this is Priscilla Wilfork. I have the lawyer's name and date of my appointment so you can send the files. At the same time can you please send me a copy of the transaction too?"

"Umm, well, hi Priscilla. I…umm…I am sorry but I have been unable to find the file of the transactions or anything to do with JemsWorld store. Everything is missing. Steven may have taken them all with him out to California. But he should have told me and I would have made a copy of it all before that. I am so sorry. He called me over a year ago and told me that he would not be coming back but I have not been able to reach him since. But I seem to remember, Priscilla, that Steven said something about another JemsWorld store being built in California as a reason why he was anxious to go out there to draw up the papers. He said he was going to make sure you were compensated for losing the store in Maine. I don't think Steven meant for you to lose out in any way. He was doing his best," Sally continued, "I will be closing the office at the end of the week but if I find out anything about the file before that I will call you. The other lawyers in the building will be available to take over all Steven's clients at that time and I will be working for them. I will let your new attorney, John Hallston, know about the missing file so you do not have to worry about it. He will contact you with further information. I wish you all the best, Priscilla. I am so sorry for everything. Take care."

"Okay, thank you, Sally. It is not your fault. There has to be some paperwork on the other end in California. The new boss would have to file for taxes. I will let the police know so they can follow up on this. Thank you for all your help, Sally. Good luck with your new job. Take care."

Priscilla hung up the phone and sighed heavily. What else was going to happen? She couldn't take much more of this. There had to be answers somewhere. She sat wringing her hands and jumped when the phone rang.

She grabbed it and breathing heavily answered, "Hello."

"Priscilla, it's Blake. Are you all right? You sound out of breath."

"Oh, Blake, I can't believe what is happening. I just got off the phone with my lawyer's secretary and she said the file of the transaction is missing. In fact, Sally told me the whole file is missing. She also said something strange. She remembers Steven telling her about a new JemsWorld store being built out in California reason why Steven was in a hurry to get out there and draw up the papers. Sally also mentioned that he wanted to make sure I was compensated for losing the Maine store and that she was sure he did his best. It is strange that he never contacted me to tell me anything about this. He also told her that he wasn't coming back here."

"Yes, he probably meant to do what was best for you. Something may have happened to him too to prevent him from calling and telling you about this whole transaction. That is why I am calling you.

Chief gave the okay for a trip to California. He is giving me three days including the time I fly out and back to complete my investigation. He thinks it is all a waste of time, but I convinced him to let me at least try to find some evidence of Parker being there. Someone had to have seen him at the hotel at least. I promise to call you as soon as I return and if I find out something of importance while I am there I will call you right away. Now, are you going to be okay while I am gone?" Blake waited anxiously for Priscilla's reply.

"Of course, I will be fine. I have to be. I have to think of Robbie first. I know you will do all you can. I will say a prayer for your safe flight back and forth and for some success while you are out there. I agree, someone must have seen Parker. How could he just disappear like that? Will Lieutenant Wholley call me if he finds out anything about Deanna while you are gone?" Priscilla's voice betrayed her as it shook with her last words of her daughter.

"Of course, Priscilla. I will fill Gus in and make sure he keeps in touch with you daily. I will be checking in with him while I am in California too. Please don't worry. We will find her. Take care of yourself and little Robbie. Talk to you soon."

"Thank you, Blake. Thank you for everything. I look forward to hearing from you. Take care and be safe too." Priscilla hung up the phone and felt exhausted mentally and emotionally. *Will Blake be able to find out what happened to Parker? Will he find Steven? Will the new boss come forward and do the right thing?* These and other questions kept surfacing in Priscilla's mind but no answers were there – yet!

***

Blake called Gus to fill him in on his trip and what he must do to keep in touch with Priscilla about anything he finds out about Deanna.

"How did you convince Chief about this trip to California? I can't believe he is going along with it. What do you think you will find out there? Do you really think that Parker Wilfork is suddenly going to come out of thin air? Don't worry, Blake I will support you and do all I can to keep Priscilla in the link of any news about Deanna, but I think this trip is a bad idea and a waste of time."

"I don't know, Gus. I can only pray that something good will come out of it. Keep looking for Deanna and follow up every lead you find. I will call you once I get to California. Call me on my cell if you find out anything at all, I mean anything! Oh, and I know, Gus. It may not be a good idea but I have to do something."

"Of course, Blake, of course. Stay safe now. Don't worry I will handle everything."

Blake left the station and headed home to pack for his trip. It would be the first time he and his son would be away from each other. Matthew would be upset but if he promised to bring him something special from out west he just might not mind staying with Mrs. Singer for a few days. She was a lovely older woman, a grandmotherly type that lived next door to Blake. She offered one day to help Blake out by staying with Matthew and had been doing it ever since his wife had died. He couldn't have continued working his schedule without her help. Blake had put Mrs. Singer in his will if something ever happened to him. She would be Matthew's caretaker and Blake would leave his house and all his money to her. Now he was wondering if that was a good idea. She was getting up in years.

Blake didn't want to think about that now. He would enjoy every minute he could with Matthew and then get this trip over with and get back to work. He had to solve this case and find Deanna. Finding Parker seemed unlikely but at least he may find out something that could tie in with Deanna's disappearance.

Matthew stormed into the house yelling, "Daddy I'm home. Daddy, where are you? Mrs. Singer told me you were home already."

"Hey, little guy! How are you? How was school today?" Blake couldn't help but smile as Matthew hugged him with his little arms as tight as he could.

"Daddy, what are you doing with your suitcase? Are we going somewhere?" Matthew's cheeks were bright pink with excitement. He loved going on a trip anywhere, even if it was just to the store. Everything was an adventure to him.

"No, sweetheart, Daddy has to go on a trip for work. But it will only be for a few days and I promise to bring something very special back for you." Blake watched his son's face as his smile disappeared and his little head dropped down in disappointment.

"Don't be sad little one. I promise we will go to MacIntosh's and get your favorite apples when I return and I also heard there is a carnival coming to town next month. I will get tickets like I did last year. Remember all the fun we had when we went last year?" Blake bent down to look at his son as he held him in his arms. He knew his leaving was going to be tough for Matthew.

"Really, Daddy? The same carnival as last year? The one with the carousel and the huge Ferris wheel? Wow, I can't wait to go on the Ferris wheel. That was so much fun, Daddy. I felt like I was flying. Didn't you too, Daddy?" Matthew's face lit up with joy as he talked on and on about the carnival much to the relief of Blake.

Mrs. Singer waved goodbye behind Matthew as she slipped out the door to give father and son some together time before Blake left in the morning.

Blake waved and said, "Thank you, Mrs. Singer. See you early tomorrow morning."

CHAPTER TWENTY-FOUR

Heading to California

Blake left the airplane and grabbed a cab to his hotel with his overnight bag slung over his shoulder. He didn't have a large expense account so he chose an inexpensive but clean hotel which was close to downtown and all the malls. It was also the same hotel that Parker had booked to stay in. This he found out from Priscilla. Blake wanted to talk to the staff and see if anyone remembered him. Priscilla didn't have much luck when she called there.

Blake's room was comfortable and it didn't take too long to get settled. He had only brought enough for a couple of days planning to leave as soon as he could. He picked up the phone on the nightstand and called home to check on Matthew.

"Hi Mary, how's Matthew doing?"

"Oh hi Sergeant Furelli. He's taking a nap. If you call back later before his bedtime I will have him talk to you then."

"Now Mary, I told you to call me Blake. Okay? That's great, I will call him later. Well, good night."

"Okay, sorry Blake. Good night."

His next call was to Gus to find out if there was any news about Deanna. "Hey, Gus, how's things going? Any news yet about Deanna?"

"Hi Blake! How was your flight? Nothing on the home front yet. But I am on top of things, don't you worry."

"Flight was okay. I couldn't sleep, too much to think about. Well, stay on top of things, partner and call me if anything comes up." Blake smiled as he talked to his partner.

"Hey, you know me, on top of things all the time, Blake! Nothing gets by me! Just you stay out of trouble out there. I am not there to take care of you," Gus chuckled at his own humor.

"Yeah, right, partner. I know how well you take care of me? Ha! Talk to you later if I find anything. Tell Chief I checked in with you so I don't have to call him too."

"Ya, sure, will do, Blake! Will do. Take care."

Blake pulled out his notepad and looked up Priscilla's cell and dialed. Her angelic face came into his mind.

"Hello," Priscilla waited on her end for an answer.

"Oh, hi Priscilla. It's Blake. I'm sorry my mind was wandering. I am in my hotel the same one as Parker. I plan to go see the manager and look around downtown for the new mega malls they have. I need to find the new JemsWorld store. Then I can locate the owner. How are you and Robbie doing?"

"We're fine, Blake. It's good to hear from you. Did you have a nice flight?"

"Yes, it was fine. I guess everyone asks that question. It was a long flight but uneventful. You sound a little tired. Are you okay?"

"Oh, I'm fine. I didn't sleep too well last night. Kept having dreams about the white angel again."

"White angel? What white angel? You didn't mention this to me before."

"Oh right, I forgot to tell you about that. I dreamt of a white angel right after Parker's disappearance and again after Deanna's. It felt like a kind presence and I didn't feel in danger at all. It was almost like I wasn't dreaming and it was really happening to me in my room. I know it sounds preposterous but I truly believe that it was Parker's spirit coming back to tell me he will watch over and protect Deanna and bring her back to me. I have prayed for something like this – a guardian angel to watch over Deanna and it happened. I felt calm and at peace after that and as if I was kissed by a butterfly. Please don't think of me as crazy or imagining things, Blake."

"No, Priscilla, I don't believe you are crazy or imagining things. I am starting to believe in guardian angels too." Blake told Priscilla about his son and the accident that took his wife.

"Oh, Blake, thank God that Matthew had a guardian angel watching over him at that time. I am so sorry about your wife. I have lost Parker but not in the same way as you lost Loriann. Please be careful out there. I look forward to having you safely back here. I will pray for your safe return. Take care, Blake. I miss you."

"I will try, Priscilla. I miss you too. Thank you for the prayers. I certainly need them. I will call you tomorrow and check in again with any news. Take care and have a good night."

"You too, Blake. Good night."

Blake hung up and realized that he really would miss Priscilla more than he could say.

Blake didn't want to waste any time and freshened up and headed to the front desk to find the manager.

Then he would get a cab to the mega mall that had a JemsWorld store.

The woman at the front desk seemed anxious as she looked at Blake when he asked to speak to the manager. She asked Blake, "Is there something I can assist you with Mr. Furelli? Is your room to your specifications?"

Blake observed the woman as she held her hands tightly together as if she was trying to keep them steady as she waited for Blake to reply.

"Everything is fine with my room. I need to speak to the manager about a private matter. He pulled out his badge and waved it in front of the desk clerk. Her eyes widen in surprise as she reached for her phone to call the manager. "Just a moment, Officer Furelli, and I will get him."

Blake didn't correct her but just nodded his head and smiled.

In a matter of seconds a tall, stately grey-haired man headed in their direction raking his fingers through his sparse hair as he spied Blake standing there looking at him.

"Are you Officer Furelli? I am Nelson Benton, manager of Hotel Los Angeles. How may I help you?"

"It is nice to meet you Mr. Benton. Yes, I am Sergeant Furelli. Thank you for meeting with me. I have a few questions to ask you about a man who came here two years ago by the name of Parker Wilfork."

Blake noticed a slight tic aside of the hotel manager's right eye as he began in an offended manner, "Excuse me Sergeant, but are you expecting me to remember every person who stayed in my hotel from over two years ago? I am sorry to disappoint you but I do not remember that name. I will have my clerk pull records from that time. What month was it? How long did Mr. Wilfork stay here?"

"I believe Mr. Wilfork was here two years ago in September. He was supposed to stay here for three days."

"Arlene, please pull the files for two years ago in September for me and bring them to my office," turning to Sergeant Furelli he directed, "Please follow me, Sergeant. Arlene will bring the files to my office and we can look them over at that time." Blake knew he was causing some unneeded interest from other guests. He hoped this would hasten the manager to give him the information more quickly.

Blake followed Mr. Benton to his office and once they were settled comfortably there was a knock at the office door.

"Come in," Mr. Benton announced as Arlene opened the door and moved into the room with a folder which she placed on her boss' desk.

Blake leaned forward and directed his attention to the folder in Mr. Breton's hands while he waited for some forthcoming information.

Mr. Benton shifted his weight and his chair groaned in protest. He didn't look heavy because of his height but the chair felt differently.

"Well, like I already told you, I do not remember any such person ever being here, Sergeant. According to my records he never came here. It looks like he cancelled his reservation that same day. He must have changed his mind about staying here. Like I told the gentleman who was here before you, Mr. Wilfork, never stayed here."

"What gentleman are you talking about, Mr. Benton? This is the first time my department has sent someone here to inquire about Mr. Wilfork." Blake knew that the Los Angeles Police Department had already been there to investigate. Funny Mr. Benton didn't mention this fact.

The tic was more prevalent in Mr. Benton's right eye and another was beginning to start by the side of his mouth. Blake kept close watch on Mr. Benton's eyes waiting for a response. He knew he was hiding something.

"It was…I don't remember the man's name but he was a PI working for Mr. Wilfork's family. I told him just what I told you, Sergeant. I am sorry I cannot help you any more than this," Mr. Benton rose from his seat as the seat once again groaned but relaxed after the weight was lifted. "Let me show you out. I have important issues to deal with now."

The tic was lessening now that Mr. Benton stopped talking and began to relax. Blake did not shake his hand and walked out of the office on his own. Next stop was to find the owner of JemsWorld store in town.

***

Unbeknownst to Blake as soon as he closed the office door Mr. Benton picked up his phone and made a call. "It's me, Nelson. I know you don't want me to call but I have some information. There was a police officer here asking about Wilfork."

"What did you tell him, Benton? I told you to throw away the files and play dumb."

"I told him Wilfork never stayed here. That is the truth. What's he going to do about that? There is no evidence of him ever being here. What else did you want me to say to him? I got rid of him quickly. He'll probably go back home and forget about Wilfork," Benton was beginning to sweat. He knew he was playing along with this man and didn't want to get him angry. Dangerous men do terrible things to those who do not go along.

"Never mind, Benton. Do not talk to him again. Do you hear me? I already took care of the Los Angeles detectives on the case through my connections with city officials. I can't do that with Maine police though." The man's voice was enough to cause a few more tics to begin pulsing away on Benton's face.

"Yes sir, I understand." Benton's hands were shaking as he replaced the phone and leaned back in his chair to think over how close he had come to death by calling this man.

***

Blake signaled for a cab as he exited the hotel and hopped in giving directions to the cabbie to go to the nearest mega mall that housed a JemsWorld store.

Blake looked out the window and noticed the skyline as they drove along. Lots of new buildings were dotting the landscape and business was booming here. He wondered who owned all these new buildings. He hadn't been to Los Angeles in several years.

"Here you are," the cabbie chirped to get his passenger's attention.

"Thanks, keep the change." Blake tipped the cabbie generously and added, "Can you come back here in half an hour to pick me up?"

"Oh, sure, half an hour it is," the cabbie smiled as he looked at the twenty in his hand.

Blake looked at the Mega Mall that sprawled out in front of him. It was quite impressive with dozens of smaller stores in the middle and flanked by four larger stores on the ends, like spokes in a wheel. He headed toward JemsWorld store. As he entered he noticed everything you could imagine in one place from food to clothes and home goods. It was a place made for one-stop shopping. Keep all the money in one place so to speak, Blake thought. Smart way to do business.

He looked for the office and found a young girl, at a counter helping several customers, wearing a nose ring and enough studs in her lip and ears to set off an alarm in an airport. He bypassed them all and leaned in with his badge on display as he asked, "Excuse me miss, I am looking for the manager."

The young girl hiccupped from fright when she spotted his badge and couldn't speak because of the cannabis she was hiding under the counter. She pointed to the hall behind her. Blake followed the corridor and soon found an office with Manager on the door. He knocked but did not get a response. Being an officer, he took a chance and turned the knob and it opened. He flicked on the light and looked around. No one was in sight. He silently closed the door and looked over the desk for any kind of paperwork that would tell him who the man was. Before he could open any drawers the office door suddenly burst open and a giant of a man stood looking at Blake with a scowl upon his huge pimpled face.

"What ya doing in here? Who do ya think you are?" the giant yelled at him.

Blake turned around and went to pull out his badge but the man was upon him before he could reach it. Blake found his hands being pulled behind his back and bent over the desk as the giant leaned into him. Seeing the giant up close and personal was not a pleasant thing to view. His breath was enough to kill a horse, maybe a whole stable.

The giant stared at him as spittle dripped onto Blake's face, "I asked you a question. Who are ya? Why are ya in Boss' office?"

Blake had to use his smarts to get out of this one and averted his face to avoid the spittle and the noxious breath. "I am a police officer and came here to investigate a case. I need to speak with your boss. I was trying to get my badge out when you accosted me. Do you know that I can arrest you for that?" Blake knew he had no jurisdiction to say this but the giant didn't know that.

Blake watched the giant's face as he seemed a little confused and startled at this little man's remark. No, Blake was not a little man, but to this giant everyone was for he stood nearly seven feet tall.

Blake's remark caused the giant to loosen his grip and relax his stance so that Blake could straighten up and put some distance between them. He felt as if he was going to pass out from the noxious gas coming from the giant's mouth most likely due to the rotting teeth.

"Listen," Blake tried to placate the giant. "I promise I won't arrest you or put in a complaint about the rough treatment on an officer of the law if you let the manager know I would like to speak with him. It should only take a few minutes of his time." Blake smiled trying to put things on a friendly basis with the imposing giant.

The giant pushed Blake aside and grunted, "Wait here and don't touch nothing!"

Blake let out a deep breath that he didn't realize he had been holding while he sat in one of the chairs facing the desk. This giant must be the manager's bodyguard. I would like to have him on my side, Blake mused.

Before Blake could prepare what he was going to ask the manager, the giant burst through the door with the manager following close behind. The imposing giant nearly blocked out the manager who stood a good foot and a half shorter than his bodyguard making Blake feel tall at six feet two inches.

Height did not mean anything when it came to the steely gaze delivered to him by the manager which made Blake now feel like a dwarf. The man's eyes were steel gray and lifeless like those of a shark. He wore an expensive silk tailored dark blue suit and slicked back dark brown hair with some gray starting to show on the sides. He moved like he was a much bigger man with an inflated ego and confidence that he could conquer anything. He was used to making the people around him watch their step and move out of his way. There was no doubt who was in charge of this store.

Before either one of them spoke, the manager reached into his drawer and pulled out a cigar, clipped it expertly with a cutter, lit it up and leaned back to observe Blake. He pointed to his giant bodyguard and whispered something and the giant moved over to stand in front of the door until he was needed.

"Now, who do I have the pleasure of meeting in front of me?" The managed aimed an alarming smile showing off brilliantly white teeth toward Blake.

"My name is Sergeant Furelli of the Leah Mills Police Department in Leah Mills, Maine. I was sent here by Chief Sangeovese to find out the whereabouts of Parker Wilfork who came to Los Angeles two years ago in September to meet with a man who wanted him to open a JemsWorld store in a mega mall." Blake was surmising that this was the reason Parker came to Los Angeles from what Priscilla had told him. Blake continued by asking, "And, you are?"

"What makes you think that I am that man? I don't know anyone by the name of Wilfork. This is my mall and my store;" he added, "my name is no business of yours. You have no jurisdiction here in California all the way from Maine."

"So you are saying that you never met with Parker Wilfork two years ago and do not know anyone by that name? Yes, I do understand that I have no jurisdiction but if I speak to the local authorities they may be interested in this case and follow through again."

"That is what I just said! I don't think that would be a good idea for you to do that!" the manager responded a little too vehemently as his eyes bored into Blake's making the officer think that he would catch fire.

"Well, I guess I have the wrong manager," Blake responded and prepared to get up to leave the office.

The manager raised his hand to the giant and he stepped away from the door but not before bumping hard into Blake and nearly knocking him off his feet as a warning.

The manager chuckled to himself and quietly reprimanded his bodyguard. "Smutty, it is not necessary to detain our guest. He is free to leave. I am sure he will not be talking to anyone about this, will you, Sergeant?" The manager met Blake with an icy stare and another warning was registered in his brain. Blake knew he had to get out of there and as quick as he could if he wanted to stay alive.

"Thank you for your hospitality," Blake replied in a more relaxed tone than he felt inside.

The manager smiled and responded back, "Have a nice flight back home," as he continued to puff on his thick cigar.

Blake didn't know where to go now but back to his hotel. It looked like he had found his man but there was no getting him to talk. He looked outside and noticed the cab waiting for him. He waved and hurried to get in and away from the danger that he had put himself in by coming there.

The cabbie looked over his shoulder and asked, "Where to now?"

Blake shuddered as he felt his nerves reacting to the recent conversation. He wanted to get out of here as quickly as he could and answered the cabbie, "Back to my hotel. I am going to the airport after I pack. Wait for me outside. I will only be a moment."

"Sure thing. I'll be here," the cabbie smiled knowing that this guy would most likely tip him nicely for the ride to the airport. The cabbie added, "You certainly are in a hurry to get away. Out-of-towners are strange people," he sighed.

CHAPTER TWENTY-FIVE

Deanna

The lock was getting loose and Deanna felt she was almost there. Jeremy had fallen asleep playing with his toys in bed. Deanna covered him up and tucked him in. She had been taking care of Jeremy for about two weeks now and had become quite close to him. Jeremy was a sweet child and so innocent. She taught him how to do simple things like pick up his toys so he wouldn't trip over them in the dark if he had to go to the bathroom. She also showed him how to print his name and spell it out loud and how to color within the lines in his coloring books. He was pleased with himself after he mastered each task.

As she thought over everything she had done over the two weeks she felt sad to leave Jeremy. Maybe she could take him with her when she escaped. He would be sad if she left without him. He was still upset over the boy who left. *I wonder if that boy ever got home. If he can escape, so can I.*

The lock gave way and Deanna opened the door and peeked around. Everything was in darkness. She waited for her eyes to adjust. She was sure the man wouldn't come home until much later. She had stayed awake one night and heard him come in at 2:00 in the morning. It was now ten. She had some time but not too much to figure out a way to get out of the house. She looked around for something heavy to break the window. There were no bars on the front windows and the drop to the sidewalk was short. She could do that but would Jeremy be able to jump?

Deanna took a close look at the lock on the front door. It was too difficult to open so she grabbed a heavy skillet and swung it as hard as she could breaking the window next to the front door. She cleared out all the glass so she could slip out but turned back at the last minute to wake up Jeremy and dress him up and take him with her. She couldn't leave him alone to get injured by the glass from the broken window.

Jeremy smiled at Deanna and blinked his eyes. He asked sleepily, "What are you doing, Ashley? It's not time to get up. Daddy hasn't come home yet, has he?"

"No, but he wants me to take you to the park. Do you want to go to the park and ride the swings?" Deanna didn't know what else to say to get him to come with her.

"Yes, I love the swings. Daddy used to take me there but we haven't been there for a long time. Can I bring Binky with me?" Binky was his stuffed zebra. Jeremy didn't go anywhere without it.

"Yes, of course, Binky can come too. Now we must hurry so we can get a swing. Ok? Be a good boy and do potty first and then I can dress you. There will be no place at the park to go potty." Deanna knew she was wasting valuable time but wanted to make sure Jeremy could walk the distance without having to go then.

Jeremy obeyed and headed toward the bathroom. Deanna could hear him flushing and then washing his hands. She had taught him well to clean up afterwards. Deanna was beginning to understand how difficult it was to be a mother.

"All done, Ashley. Can I wear my jeans and my dinosaur shirt?"

"Yes, sure, Jeremy. Now we must hurry. We have to walk to the park and it is a little way from here."

Deanna had no idea where the park was but would improvise as they went along and would get as far away from the man's house before stopping to ask for help from a neighbor.

Ashley bundled Jeremy up with a coat and a hat since it was a little chilly out and she grabbed her own coat as she went to the front door. She brush away the broken glass from the window frame and floor with a broom she found in the corner and told Jeremy she would go first. He looked at her and asked, "Why are we going out the window, Ashley?"

"I can't open the front door, Jeremy. This is the only way we can go out. Now, you stay right here and I will catch you when you come out. Deanna jumped down into the bushes which wasn't too bad. The thick bushes cushioned her fall. Now she put her arms out to Jeremy as he sat on the window sill and looked down at her.

"I don't know how to jump, Ashley," Jeremy said in a frightened voice.

"I promise I will catch you. Just lean out and make believe you are flying." This definitely did the trick because the next second Jeremy was falling into her arms and both of them plopped into the bushes.

The angel watched over Deanna and cushioned the fall of both her and Jeremy as they made their escape out the window. He followed the children as they walked down the street keeping a safe distance above the streetlights so that they would not see him.

Jeremy was laughing as he asked, "Can I do that again, Ashley? That was fun."

"No, once is quite enough, Jeremy. Let's get going to the park. Okay?" Deanna grabbed Jeremy's hand and led him away from the house.

"I know how to get to the park, Ashley. It is this way," Jeremy pulled Deanna in the opposite direction.

"No, I think it is this way, Jeremy. Come on now we must hurry." Deanna looked around the dark and empty streets for an escape route. Houses were not too close together here but there were street lights and she followed along from one light to another as she got to the end of the block pulling Jeremy along. He seemed like he was going to fall asleep. Poor thing he was tired and not used to being up this late. Jeremy nearly lost Binky as he stumbled along beside Deanna.

Deanna didn't know what to do at this point. She kept pulling Jeremy along and hoping that a car would come by and she could ask for help. She would try the house at the next corner maybe they would help her get home.

The Angel waited until he was sure the children were safe then went back to the broken window and bent down and looked through the bushes.

CHAPTER TWENTY-SIX

Manager's Office in California

The man stood at attention as he listened to his boss give him instructions. He would do anything for his boss and had proven on multiple occasions to be very resourceful.

"Follow him to his hotel and make sure he gets on the plane. I don't want him back here again. Do you understand, Smutty?"

"Oh, yes sir, I will make sure he leaves. Do you want me to put him away so he can't talk?"

"No Smutty. He is expected to return home. If he doesn't, there will be others to follow him. You already took care of the owner of the store, his lawyer and one PI. I think that is quite enough for now. We have nowhere else to bury them. I would have to put up another building," Byron chuckled thinking back at what he had gotten away with so far. He didn't want to take any chances killing a cop though. Nothing good would come out of that.

Smutty smiled thinking of the fun he had putting down the three guys. He enjoyed pulling the trigger but really didn't need to do that. He could have just picked them up and thrown them into the pit and that would have killed them easy enough.

"Smutty, are you listening to me? Now get on back to the hotel. Benton will call when the cop gets back to the hotel. I want you to watch him get on a plane and leave. You understand. Nothing else needs to be done."

"Sure boss. Just watch him get on a plane and fly away. I can do that."

After Smutty left his office Byron thought it might be a good idea to check in on Priscilla's daughter. He had plans to threaten to kidnap her to send a warning to Priscilla not to follow up with this wild goose chase to find her husband or the man he met. He knew she would go to the police immediately and would stop the police from doing anything further in fear of her daughter's life. After all she had already lost a husband. She wouldn't want to lose a daughter too.

***

Blake was in line to change his ticket when he noticed the giant watching him from the back of the terminal. It was hard not to see him. He stood out like a dinosaur would strolling Central Park. He was nearly as big, Blake thought chuckling to himself.

All Blake wanted to do was get back home and see his son and Priscilla. He missed them both. Funny how he was already thinking of them as being a family. Matthew would love having a brother and a sister. As soon as he thought of sister his mind went to Deanna. He only hoped some more evidence came out of his talking with little Peter Carter. Maybe Peter would remember something else now about the man or the house. Blake would call the Carters again right after seeing his son. Of course, he would check in with the chief first then head home.

If he had to, he would call Chief Sangeovese at his home. It was three hours difference at home and the chief would be in bed most likely when he arrived in Maine. But Blake felt this was important enough to disturb him.

Blake rested his head back on the headrest and fell asleep. When he awoke they were pulling into the terminal in Millbury, Maine. He had left his car in the lot and would drive the rest of the way home to Leah Falls which was forty minutes away.

The drive was calming to Blake as it felt good to be home. Los Angeles was beautiful but too glitzy and crowded for him. He couldn't live there. He would miss the country and the warmth and kindness of the people around him.

He turned on his phone and dialed the chief's house to see if he could give him a heads-up that he was heading that way. A groggy voice came on the line. "Whoever this is better have a good reason for disturbing my beauty sleep!"

"Hi Chief, it's me, Sergeant Furelli. I am on my way to your house and need to speak with you. It's urgent."

"Blake, what the hell are you doing back so soon? I gave you three days. Don't tell me you solved all the problems in a matter of hours?"

"Well, not really, Chief, but what I need to tell you will be a surprise."

"Can't it wait until morning, Sergeant? The world is not coming to an end over this, is it?" Chief was using his usual acerbic tone meant to discourage any more dialogue.

"No, but you will want to hear what I have found out. Pulling into your drive now, Chief."

***

Chief rubbed his eyes and sat up, clearly unhappy about missing his eight hours of sleep but Blake was one of his best officers and would not call unless it was important. For Blake's sake, Chief thought, it better be important.

Chief grabbed his bathrobe and headed to his front door as the bell sounded. Blake didn't waste any time but strode in past the chief and sat down on his couch and made himself comfortable as he waited for Chief Sangeovese to sit down. Blake turned to the chief and filled him in on all the details leaving nothing out including the description of the giant bodyguard. He even displayed his bruises on his chest from the giant much to the dismay of Chief Sangiovese.

"Okay, I see that this is disturbing. But what can I do to this guy? We are clearly out of our jurisdiction. The Los Angeles Police Department already investigated things out there and found nothing. The case is closed now. Well… I could call a friend of mine out there but I really don't have anything to give him. There is no proof of this man even meeting Wilfork except the fact that he now owns Parker's store. Even the hotel, as you say, did not see him. He never showed up there. All right, let me stew about this and tomorrow we will talk more. Get home and get some sleep. I expect you in bright and early tomorrow. Goodnight, oh, and it's good to have you back. Gus missed you!" Chief Sangeovese laughed at the expression of amusement on Blake's face at the mention of his partner.

Blake let himself out of Chief Sangeovese's house and headed home. There really wasn't anything he could do at this point, he agreed. There would be a lot more to discuss when he got into the station tomorrow. But for now he would go home and try to get some sleep. He looked forward to seeing Matthew first thing in the morning. It would be a nice surprise for him to be home early even if he didn't have a gift for him. Blake would have to come up with something but for the time being his son wouldn't even remember the gift when he saw his father.

Blake's head hit the pillow and was lights out. The time change had really gotten to him. The next thing he remembered was Matthew's excited voice yelling, "Daddy's home, Daddy's home! Wake up Daddy!"

CHAPTER TWENTY-SEVEN

New Developments

Carl Hemp was at work unaware what was taking place at his house in the middle of the night. He had been busy working in the warehouse of JemsWorld store cleaning up some spills from one of the soup boxes that had fallen and spilled out. The powder was pure white and did not look like any soup he had ever seen. Carl bent down and touched the powder and sniffed and put a grain on his tongue. Wow, it was not soup, he thought out loud. He was so involved with the powder that he didn't notice someone standing nearby watching him. By the time he took notice there was a gun being held to side of his head. He didn't dare move to look at the man holding the gun. *What is this man doing in the warehouse with a gun? Why is he holding it to my head?*

Carl managed to take a quick peek and stared at the man. He had never seen this man before. Carl tried to speak but the man pushed the gun tighter against his temple. As he was pushing Carl along another man came forward and yelled at the man holding the gun. "What are you doing? Are you crazy or something? Now he saw you? The boss didn't say to get involved with the store help. He is not going to be happy about this. We can't waste any time, just shoot him. We need to get to the airport with the shipment."

"Stop yelling at me. I know what to do. Get off my case, will ya?" the man holding the gun said taking his eyes off of Carl to address his anger toward the second man.

The two men argued back and forth giving Carl enough time to make a run for it. He knew all the exits especially the ones no one else used except him on his rounds to empty the trash. Carl headed for the closest hidden exit and rushed through the door before the first shot went off over his head.

Once outside he kept running through the parking lot and into the next lot through high grass. Carl quickly dropped down in the grass to hide as the two men came out of the warehouse looking for him. They looked in all directions then headed back to the store to get their vehicle.

Carl peeked through the grass and saw his chance to run and keep running for his life. He ran through to the next street and headed to a house which was protected by some large trees from the street. He knocked loudly on the door and waited for someone to answer. A man looked out through the peephole at him and opened the door with the chain still attached. Carl pleaded with the man, "Please call the police and let me come in. Someone is after me with a gun," Carl anxiously tried to relay that his life was in danger.

The man left the door and came back with a cell phone and handed it to Carl who dialed 911 as his hands violently shook. As soon as the call was connected Carl yelled, "Help, please help me. I am at…Landers Court behind JemsWorld store and someone chased me with a gun. I am the janitor at the store and someone is trying to kill me. Please hurry. They'll be coming."

The man behind the door who was listening opened it and pulled Carl in. He looked out to make sure no one had seen Carl before abruptly closing the door. He told Carl, who was still holding the phone in his shaky hand, "Please sit down. Sorry I didn't know what to think when I saw you standing there. I didn't know who you were. If you work at JemsWorld then you are all right by me. Mr. Wilfork wouldn't hire any hooligans for his store. Sit tight and I will get you some whiskey to take the edge off. I can't imagine what it feels like to have someone chasing you with a gun. My name's Fred, be right back." Fred relieved Carl of the phone and headed out to his kitchen.

Carl let out a huge sigh of relief as he looked forward to having a whiskey. He was frightened out of his mind. If something happened to him, what would happen to Jeremy?

Fred came back with two glasses of whiskey and offered one to Carl as the front door bell rang. Fred looked through the peephole to make sure it was the police before opening it. Lieutenant Wholley stood there showing his badge and stepped in as Carl drank down the whiskey in one gulp.

Fred offered Lieutenant Wholley some too, "No thank you, I am on duty. I need to speak with this gentleman alone for a moment. What is your name?"

"Oh, Fred's my name. Sure, I will be out in the kitchen."

Carl's eyes were wide and glassed over from the whiskey but his hands were shaky and he tried to hold them still in his lap as he waited to explain his unnerving experience to the officer.

Gus looked at the man as he watched him try to keep his nerves in control and asked, "What is your name?"

Carl looked anxiously at the policeman as he tried to find his voice, "Carl Hemp."

"Please start from the beginning, Carl, and tell me what happened tonight."

"Well, I was at work at JemsWorld store on night shift. I work from 6:00 pm to 2:00 am in the warehouse at the back of the store. I was cleaning up some spills that were supposed to be soup but were anything but. Around 1:00 am (I had looked at my watch shortly before this) I felt a gun being held to my head. Another man came forward and the two men started arguing about what they were going to do with me. I ran while they were preoccupied and came to the first house I could to call for help." Carl took a deep breath and looked at his empty glass desperately in need of a refill.

"Can you describe the two men?" Gus looked closely at Carl to make sure he was still lucid after his drink. He was frightened and definitely looking a little lost.

"Yes, I can. They were both beefy guys and bigger than me in height and weight. I caught a glimpse of them as they were arguing. One guy was bald and the other had unruly brown hair. Officer, I need to go home to my son. Do I need to go to the station?"

"Yes I would like you to come to the station to look at some photos and describe these two men to one of our artists. We need to get their faces out there. You can call home to check on your son from there."

"Hold on one minute, Carl." Lieutenant Wholley called into the station to report the present situation at the warehouse store and the two men at large.

"No I need to go home. He is…umm. All right, officer," Carl didn't continue, afraid of giving away the fact that his son was not with an adult. He didn't want the officer to check on his son and find the girl.

Gus went out to the kitchen and told Fred he was leaving with Carl, "Thank you, Fred, for being a good neighbor and letting Carl stay here until I could come get him. Your cooperation is appreciated. Good night. If you hear anything strange or see these men call the station right away."

"Of course, Officer. I certainly will. Just trying to do my part. Take it easy, Carl."

Carl waved to Fred and followed Lieutenant Wholley to his vehicle. His mind was spinning as he thought over what had transpired and how close he had come to dying. He had to do something about protecting his son. He made up his mind to let Deanna go and get help for his son.

Gus called into the station to report he was on his way back with Carl Hemp, janitor of JemsWorld store.

It had been a long night for Gus. He was pulling double duty to cover for Blake. There were two other officers doing mornings but things were busier lately on nights with minor disturbances and kids getting out of hand on street corners. His nights had kept him hopping. Now with two men running around with guns. He couldn't wait until Blake came back.

He got back to the station and was surprised to see the chief sitting at his desk. He wasn't expected in until later in the morning. Gus rolled his eyes and pulled Carl along with him and sat him down next to his desk as he headed over to talk to Chief Sangeovese.

"Hey, Gus, get over here. Blake came back and will be here in at 7:00 am. I need to fill you in."

***

The two gun men were riding up and down the streets looking for the janitor shortly after Carl hid out in Fred's house. Once the two men saw the police car they headed back to the warehouse and finished packing the truck to be taken to the Millbury Regional Airport. Their boss needed to have the packages sent to Chicago as soon as possible.

They knew what the boss would do to them if they reported a problem in the warehouse at JemsWorld. They drove as quickly as possible to the airport carefully staying under the speed limit so that they wouldn't be stopped. If they did not arrive at the airport on time, their lives were going to be in jeopardy. Two police cars passed them heading back toward the store. By the looks of things the janitor had reported their confrontation with him.

The driver looked over at his passenger with a deep feeling of angst, "Ralph, now you have done it. What do you think the boss is going to do to us? We had things going smoothly without police interference. We were to keep everything under the radar."

"Hey, Buzz, the janitor was hanging around the package and was sniffing around the stuff that spilled. I couldn't let him find out about the drugs."

"But you didn't have to pull your gun. You could have done it diplomatically and just told him to go clean another place until we were finished loading," Buzz muttered to himself, "I need to call the boss and let him know we are on our way to the airport without telling him about the police. But maybe I will wait, the less he knows the better."

"You had better push the pedal to the metal a little harder or we will never get there, Buzz." Ralph was thinking about what he was going to do once they delivered the goods. He planned on getting out of town pronto. He had stashed some money in his room and was going to collect it and get on another plane after the delivery and head to the Bahamas. He let out a sigh as he looked out the window.

CHAPTER TWENTY-EIGHT

At Millbury Regional Airport the plane was revving up in anticipation of the arrival of the shipment. The men pushed forward on the gas as they saw the plane on the runway ahead. They screeched to a halt jumping out and opening the car doors to start unloading. The last package was put on board and the men followed and took their seats as the plane started to taxi down the runway.

Chief Sangeovese had called the airport after Lieutenant Wholley told him what Carl Hemp had reported about the gunmen going to the airport. Chief talked to the airport supervisor to stop any private planes from leaving the terminal until the police could check out the questionable cargo.

Chief Sangeovese had sent two cars to check out the warehouse first and then check back with him before proceeding. The police pulled up to the warehouse and releasing their guns headed for the door. The door was still opened and they looked around as they flicked on the lights. Boxes were haphazardly stacked and not in any particular order looking like the place had been ransacked by someone in a hurry.

The police moved through the rest of the store to ensure no one was hiding. Going back to their vehicles they called in to Chief Sangeovese, "Officer Jongas here. Officer Gregory and I just checked out the warehouse and store, all clear. Where do you want us to go now?"

"Go to the airport – Millbury Regional Airport, and fast. The men may be on their way there. I already called the airport supervisor to hold the plane until you can check out the cargo. I want to know what is in them. We have reports that there may be something illegal going on. Don't do anything else when you get there but keep them from flying that plane. I called the Feds and they are on their way there to take over."

"Yes sir, Chief. We're heading there now."

With sirens sounding the two squad cars headed toward the airport just as the plane was taxiing down the runway. The police pulled out their guns and shot at the tires to stop the plane. They drove their cars right up to the plane and cut it off. There was a screeching of tires as the plane swerved and nearly tipped forward nose first and crashed into the police cars.

Meanwhile on the plane, Buzz hearing the pilot say they were not cleared to take off pulled out his gun and held it to the pilot's head and yelled, "Take off now or I shoot you."

With guns drawn the police officers approached the plane and called out, "Open up or we will shoot."

The hatch opened and out filed the co-pilot and a stewardess with their hands up. The pilot, however, was unable to leave the plane because of the gun being held to his head.

***

Byron sat back and lit another cigar. He pulled out his cell and called Smutty. Byron planned to have Smutty get in touch with Buzz and Ralph back at the warehouse in Maine if they had not left yet to head to the airport with the shipment. He wanted them to come right back after dropping off the shipment in Chicago to keep a closer eye on the girl. When they saw a chance, they were to grab her and put her in a backroom of the warehouse and keep her heavily sedated until he told them what to do next.

The men were close to the girl being in the same town and had taken turns sitting outside the girl's school to keep an eye on her already. This daring move was to put a halt to any more questions directed towards him from Priscilla or the police.

Smutty reported to his boss promptly and got Ralph on the phone after Buzz's phone went to voicemail.

"Listen Ralph, the boss requested I call you about picking up the Wilfork girl. The daughter of the former owner of the store, you know who I mean," Smutty was getting testy with Ralph who didn't seem to be listening to him. "Where are you right now? What's that noise in the background? Who's yelling? Was that gunshots?" Smutty looked alarmed as he met his boss' eye.

Buzz looked at Ralph and mouthed, "What did Boss say?" while he kept his eye on the door of the plane when he heard gunshots.

Ralph turned to Buzz and mouthed back, "He wants us to kidnap the girl at the school, the store owner's little girl," Ralph reported as he turned his attention back to his phone. He hadn't noticed Buzz disappearing behind him.

Byron's ears perked up when he heard Smutty say, gunshots. "Give me that phone now!" He ripped it out of Smutty's big mitt and yelled, "What the hell is going on over there? You better have a good explanation. Did you get the shipment out yet?" Byron tapped the end of his cigar and broke it off when Ralph answered.

"We…umm…are in the plane now taxiing but two cop cars just cut us off. They just shot at the tires. The cops are boarding the plane. I…."

Another voice came on the phone and identified himself as Officer Jongas after Ralph handed over his phone to the officer when the policeman's gun appeared in his face. Ralph could see his escape to a sunny location was now out of reach. He wasn't going to take the brunt of the blame for this fiasco he thought as he looked around for Buzz who was nowhere in sight.

Three dark SUVs pulled up as the officers held their guns drawn at the plane and its inhabitants. What they didn't see was one man crawling out of the bottom of the plane and running away.

***

Byron didn't answer but instead abruptly hung up the phone and threw it against the wall where it broke into pieces severing the connection and any way the police could find him.

Byron pulled out his bottom drawer where there was a passport and money he had set aside for a time like this. He called Ned and instructed him to bring the limo to his office immediately. He next called the airline to fly out of L.A. Airport and booked a flight to Switzerland by way of Toronto, Canada without a stop which should take about seven hours or so. It was leaving within the hour.

He shook hands with Smutty and shoved a pack of thousands into his hand as he grabbed his briefcase which he had filled with his money, passport and an untraceable phone.

Byron ran out of the office before Smutty could say thank you. Smutty planned on making himself scarce too which would now be a lot easier.

Ned was sitting outside and jumped out to open the door when his boss came out of his office building. He knew by the look on his boss' face that the fateful day must have arrived when he would be out of a job and the boss would be on the run. He turned toward the boss and asked, "Where to, Boss?"

Byron responded in a brisk tone, "LA Airport now and hurry, Ned," then added calmly, "Thank you, Ned, for all you have done. I will send your remaining salary directly to your account."

Boss then handed Ned a stack of thousands as he had done for Smutty before sitting back to collect his thoughts.

***

Buzz took advantage of the attentions of the officers being diverted by the SUVs coming along. He ran over to his car, a green Ford, which was sitting with its trunk still opened. He quickly shut it and started the engine, backing up and pulling away from the plane. The SUVs were still a short distance from the plane and may not have noticed him. He planned to call Boss and tell him what happened and that he needed some funds to get away. But first he planned to pick up some insurance before he left. The boss wanted him to kidnap the girl. If he could get her the boss would be happy to reward him handsomely in a monetary way.

CHAPTER TWENTY-NINE

After Chief filled Gus in about California, Lieutenant Wholley went back over to Carl Hemp who was sitting there with his head in his hands. He had kept Carl sitting there for well over an hour and a half while he waited for the sketch artist to get there. Gus had spent a good part of that time with Chief discussing Carl's complaint of two armed men chasing him. Chief had contacted the Feds and things were moving fast. Gus sighed as he thought, Blake would be coming in a few hours.

Directing his attention back to the man sitting by his desk, Gus asked, "Well, Carl Hemp, what do you say for yourself?" Lieutenant Wholley raised his voice in order to get Carl's attention. His eyes were glassy and had a faraway look like he wasn't even there. This man is definitely holding back something, Gus surmised.

"Yes, Officer? I am just worried about my son. I need to get home. He will be waking up around 6:00 am and wonder where I am." Carl looked at his watch. It was already going on 4:30 am and the officer hadn't even asked him any questions about his statement yet.

"Well, let's get started now." Gus informed Carl that he had called for one of their artists to come in early to draw up a sketch of the two gun men. The sketch artist now sat down next to Carl and set up his pad with pencil poised ready to begin. The precinct still didn't have the funds to purchase the computer or the newest technology to do the sketching to go with it. It was on back order like most things in this small town.

Carl repeated what he had already told Gus at Fred's house and added again, "Lieutenant, please I need to get home right away. It is getting late. My son needs me."

After another hour the artist had his sketch. Gus nodded and brought it over to Chief Sangeovese.

"Great, get copies of this out to all officers and one to neighboring police stations. The Feds have one in custody but the other perp is still at large.

"Are you finished with the witness, Gus? If you are, take him home. I called in for more officers from other stations. They are out now combing the area for the other man. Once Blake gets here I want you to go home to rest. In fact, Gus, why don't you take the witness home and then head home yourself. I don't need you to drop from exhaustion," Chief looked at his officer and could see the strain on his face. Gus was getting up there in age and Chief didn't want to push him too far. Gus was due to retire in the next year or sooner by the looks of him.

"I don't want to see you here. Take the day off. Your buddy is back now which will make your life easier," Chief laughed at Gus' surprised expression. "Yes, I did say take the day off, now go."

"Okay, Chief, will do. Thanks, it's been a long night."

Carl looked relieved when Gus told him, "Well, it looks like you got your wish, Carl. Chief requested I take you home. Now you can check on your son."

"Oh, thank you very much, Officer, I mean Lieutenant Wholley. I appreciate that," Carl responded relieved to be finally going home. He hoped that Ashley was taking good care of Jeremy.

Carl gave Gus his address and leaned forward as they drove down each street. As they were getting closer to his house Carl let out a breath that he didn't realize he was holding.

Gus heard the deep exhale from Carl and couldn't figure out why he was so anxious. His wife or sitter was there surely watching over his son.

Carl tried the handle of the vehicle but found it locked. "Can you let me out now Lieutenant Wholley?"

"Just a moment Carl. Would you like me to come in with you? You seem a little too nervous over what has happened to you. You need to calm down or you will upset your son. How old is he?"

"He is four and has special needs."

"Oh, I see. Well, if you don't need me to come in with you I will let you off and head home."

Carl jumped out as soon as the lock was disengaged and ran up the stairs to his house. Just as he was putting in the key he noticed the broken window. He unlocked the door, pushed his way in quickly and ran into his son's room which was wide open. He looked in the bathroom and called out to both children with no response. He ran around the house looking into all the rooms but finding no sign of them.

Gus was sitting outside and noticed Carl's sudden rush into the house. He got out of the squad car and went up the stairs to see what had upset Carl. He noticed the broken window and immediately radioed the station. His night was not over yet.

"Carl, what's going on? Where is your son?" Gus stood in the living room looking around as Carl ran helter-skelter back and forth looking for his son.

Gus stopped Carl as he ran by him, "Who was here with your son? Your wife or a sitter?"

"I had a sitter, umm…I mean his sister…umm," Carl stammered not knowing what to say.

"Carl, you need to give me a description of your son and his sitter or sister, which is it?" Gus was clearly confused by this man's erratic behavior.

"My son has Down Syndrome. He can't be out on his own."

"What about the sitter? Can you give me a description?"

"She is about eight years old and has bl..., I mean …"

"You mean to tell me you don't know what the girl looks like?" Gus gave Carl a look of incredulity.

Gus relayed the message and description of the little boy and lack of one of the sitter to the precinct.

"Listen Carl, are you going to be all right? I need to canvas the neighborhood and see if your son and his sitter wandered away or just went for a walk."

"Can I come with you, Lieutenant? I need to find Jeremy. He doesn't know his way home if he gets lost. He is never out on his own," Carl asked as his eyes filled up and he trembled all over.

"No, you need to stay here in case he comes home. Go make yourself some coffee and I will call you as soon as I find him."

"But, Lieutenant, I need to…."

"Carl, go sit by the phone and get that coffee in you. You have had a disturbing night. I will do all I can to find your son."

Gus' head was spinning with the two cases crossing back and forth. He felt like he was missing something about what Carl had told him. He would have to go back over his statement and review it. Something wasn't right.

CHAPTER THIRTY

A Strange Call

Priscilla woke up early as usual to prepare breakfast for herself and Robbie. She let Robbie sleep in until the last minute. He seemed tired last night and was restless. He kept calling out Deanna's name in his sleep. The poor baby, she thought, he must really miss his sister.

Before she could wake Robbie up the phone rang and she quickly picked it up so as not to disturb her son. She listened as her caller articulated, "Mrs. Wilfork, I presume. I want you to stop sending out people to find your husband. You will never find him. Now I think you should be carefully watching your daughter or she may disappear like her father did. Tell the cops to stay away or your daughter will not be around much longer."

Priscilla was in shock as the caller clicked off. She couldn't even respond to what the caller had said about her daughter. Now she knew that this man was responsible for her Parker's disappearance. But he didn't sound like he knew that Deanna was already missing. If he didn't take her then who did?

She looked for the numbers that Blake had left her and dialed his cell. She knew that it was three hours difference out there but he should be out doing his investigation.

Priscilla, anxiously tapping her foot, waited for Blake to pick up. She was about to leave a message when she heard his voice.

"Priscilla, I was just going to call you. What's wrong? Why are you crying?"

"Oh Blake, I just received a call from the man who…who took Parker away from me. Now he is threatening to take Deanna. He said if I didn't call off the cops he would make sure Deanna disappeared like Parker did. Could he have Deanna? He didn't sound like he knew she was already missing though when he threatened me. What are we going to do? How will I ever find her? Oh Blake, I'm so frightened for my poor baby girl. I swear he or whoever has Deanna better not hurt her in any way."

"I am coming over there right now. I will report to Chief Sangeovese what you told me and be there soon. Just sit tight. I will get to the bottom of this, I promise you."

Blake found himself shaking but by pulling himself together he became angry. *This man can't bully everyone like this, especially an innocent little girl.*

If I get my hands on him, without his bodyguard around, I will wring his neck.

Priscilla wiped her tears and went to get Robbie up. She needed to get him to school but she was nervous to let him out of her sight. *Blake had to have a way to solve this. She had to get her daughter back. This man's tentacles spread out all the way to Maine. He must have people here watching us. I wish Parker had never gone to California. He opened up a hornet's nest. Blake just stirred the hornets more. Oh, dear Go,d please watch over Deanna, she cried.*

Robbie snuggled up to his mother as she tried to wake him up and dress him for school. She carried him out to the kitchen and set him down in his booster seat to eat his breakfast. She watched him lovingly with tears in her eyes as she thought of Deanna. How would she survive if something happened to her? She shook herself and tried to smile at Robbie as he watched her expressions with concern. He knew something was wrong and had upset his mother.

"Mommy why are you sad? Is Deanna coming home yet? I miss her, Mommy. I want her to come home."

"I am sad that she isn't home too, Robbie. But I promise she will be coming home soon. Now finish up your breakfast so I can take you to school."

Priscilla called Blake to tell him to wait at the house for her to come back from dropping off Robbie. She didn't want him to leave if he got there before she returned.

***

Blake sat outside Priscilla's house waiting for her to come back home. He couldn't think of anything to say to her about finding Deanna. They still did not have any clue. Peter Carter had not been able to provide a good description of his abductor other than he had brown hair. Blake had hoped that Peter would be able to give him something more than that. He knew that Peter was too young to realize where he was taken. Peter did say it was far from home. It was a miracle that the boy found his way to the playground near his home. Peter must have a guardian angel too, Blake mused.

Blake's thoughts were interrupted as he got a call from dispatch about a woman reporting finding a little boy and a girl walking alone on her street. She had taken them in and was waiting for the police to come and pick them up.

Blake got the address and sped away. As he was driving away he passed Priscilla. He waved and held up his mike to show he was on a call.

Blake put on his siren and floored it until he reached the address. He ran up the stairs to the front door and prepared to knock but the door was opened by an older woman who seemed relieved to see him. She welcomed him into her house and brought him into her living room where two children slept soundly on her couch wrapped in blankets. The little boy held onto a stuffed zebra and the little girl was snuggled next to the little boy.

Blake called the station and reported finding the children. The girl he suspected was Deanna but he was not sure of who the boy could be.

He felt a great relief as he watched the children sleeping without a care in the world. He listened to the older woman who identified herself as Mrs. Porter.

"I looked out of my front window. I don't usually sleep through the night and saw two small shapes walking in front of my house. I opened the door and called to them. The girl was holding onto the little boy's hand protectively. I couldn't figure out why they were wandering around this early in the morning. I went out to talk to them and brought them in. They were exhausted and fell promptly to sleep as soon as they laid down. I called the police once they fell asleep."

"What did they say to you about being out by themselves at this time of the morning?" Blake queried.

"The young girl told me that she needed to go home to her mother and brother. The little boy she had with her evidently was not her brother but he thought he was. He called her Ashley. But she told me that her name was Deanna."

"Okay, I see. Thank you for taking them in. We have been looking for the girl but I don't know who the boy is. I will take care of them from now on. I hate to wake them up but I need to bring them to the police station."

"I am happy to help, Officer. I am a grandmother and my heart goes out to these dear children and their parents who are probably wondering where they are."

"Don't worry, Mrs. Porter, the children are safe now and will be home with their families soon. Now I need to wake the children." Blake bent over and gently touched Deanna's shoulder. He was rewarded with a sweet smile from Deanna who shook the little boy to wake him too.

CHAPTER THIRTY-ONE

Back at the Station

Chief was busy with the news of the two children being found. He called Gus and told him to get back to the station immediately for Blake had found the little boy that he was looking for only two blocks away from his house.

Gus went back to Carl Hemp's house and picked him up to bring him back to the station to identify his son. He knew Carl would be relieved to hear his son was safe.

"Carl, we found your son with a young girl. Is she the one who was taking care of him?" Gus looked closely at Carl for some response.

"Well, umm…well…I…sorry Lieutenant. I need to explain. You don't understand my wife died two months ago and I am alone with no other family that are local. What else was I going to do?"

"So you admit to kidnapping the girl? Did you know that kidnapping could be a federal offense?" Gus neglected to add if done across state lines. Not waiting for Carl to answer, Gus added, "We will decide what to do about you when we get to the station. You will have to answer for this."

Gus had been told that the girl in question was Deanna who had been missing for two weeks.

Carl Hemp admitted, "I…I'm sorry but I did pick up the girl but I didn't hurt her. It was only going to be temporary until I could get some help."

"I can't believe you! What were you thinking to kidnap children to use as babysitters?" Something was definitely wrong with this man! Gus thought sadly.

CHAPTER THIRTY-TWO

Happy Reunion

Blake arrived at the station with two still sleepy children as Gus pulled up behind him with Carl Hemp in tow.

Blake assisted the children out of the vehicle and escorted them into the station as Carl Hemp ran closely behind trying to catch up to his son who was yet unaware his father was there.

As soon as the children were settled down Blake ordered some breakfast for them to be delivered from a diner nearby. After he made sure the children were okay he called Priscilla to report the good news.

Things had been happening so fast that he never did get back to talk to her about her phone call but nothing was as important as finding Deanna. Blake waited for Priscilla to pick up as he observed the children eating their breakfast. Carl Hemp sat next to his son with his arm protectively around his son's shoulder while the other hand was handcuffed to the desk. Deanna helped the little boy with his straw and opened his carton of milk for him like a little mother.

Blake headed out to his vehicle and called Priscilla as he drove. "Hi Priscilla....

"Blake, thank God, I was worried. You never came back. Is everything okay?"

"Priscilla, I have good news for you," Blake waited for Priscilla to register what he just told her.

"What, what did you say, Blake? News, what news?"

"We found Deanna, Priscilla. We found her! She is fine. I am on my way over to pick you up. We want you here before we can ask her any questions." Blake headed out to the squad car and drove over to Priscilla's house as he spoke with her.

"Oh God, Blake! You found her! I...oh my God! You found her! I can come to the station. I can't wait any longer. I can't believe it! Are you sure she is okay? What did she say? Where has she been?"

"Please Priscilla, don't worry. We will find out all we can. The most important thing is that Deanna is safe and sound. I'm pulling up at your house now."

Priscilla came running out of her house as Blake was pulling up. She held onto her coat, pocketbook and keys and rushed forward to the squad car as Blake came out to open up the door for her.

***

Gus was keeping an eye on the kids. As they were enjoying their breakfast he glanced once again at Carl Hemp's statement.

He scanned carefully over each sentence he had typed but stopped when he came to one about the substance found on the floor of the warehouse. Gus jumped up and ran over to Chief's office to report what he thought he had clearly missed.

Gus knocked on his Chief's door as he shifted his weight to his left knee. The right one was aching today for being on his feet all night.

Chief looked up after hanging up his phone and motioned for Gus to come in.

"What's up Gus? Something wrong?" Chief Sangeovese could see the worry lines on Gus's face deepen as he prepared to tell him something.

"Well, Chief, I apologize but I just realized that I missed what Carl Hemp mentioned in his statement about the warehouse. He stated that he found a substance on the floor which was spilled soup or was supposed to be spilled soup. But, however, it was not soup but a white substance – drugs – possibly cocaine. Carl reported that he smelled it and tasted a little on the tip of his tongue." Gus watched Chief for any sign that he was in trouble for just remembering this important information.

"Thanks Gus, but I already called the officers and they are at the airport to stop the shipment. I figured as such when I read Carl's statement and also suspected that from the late night shipments. Don't worry, Lieutenant. I know how tired you are. You did not miss anything. You did give me a heads up about that already when we spoke earlier. You don't remember? Believe me, if you did miss anything I would be the first to blast you for it!"

"Now start the investigation by talking to the children. Did Blake come back with Mrs. Wilfork yet?" Chief's phone rang causing him to ignore Gus's response as he gave the caller all his attention.

"Okay, Chief, thanks. No, but I am sure she is anxious to get here to see her daughter." Gus slipped out of Chief's office as he heard the sound of clicking heels. Entering the room was Priscilla Wilfork who ran towards her daughter.

"Deanna, sweetheart!" Priscilla yelled as she pulled her daughter into a tight hug.

"Mommy, I missed you! I'm sorry for not being nice to you. Are you angry with me?" Deanna's tear-streaked face looked up to meet her mother's equally wet face.

"Oh no, dear child. I could never be angry with you. Everything is fine now that you are back. Are you okay? Did anyone hurt you?"

Hearing this exchange, Blake hurried over to listen in on the conversation before Deanna could answer. He pulled up a chair and sat down next to mother and daughter as they cried in each other's arms patiently waiting for a chance to talk to Deanna.

CHAPTER THIRTY-THREE

Filling in the Blanks

Blake looked over at Gus who was slumped in his chair and snoozing at his computer. He had a long night and had not slept in more than a day. He felt guilty for leaving his old partner to deal with all the problems that had come up in the short time he was away in California. It was a wasted trip. But he did find out what a dangerous man the new owner of JemsWorld could be. LA police would have to keep an eye on him. He was bound to trip up somewhere.

Blake had spoken to Deanna and she had told him all he needed to know about her kidnapping and the man who took her, Carl Hemp. Carl would be locked away until his trial to face the charges for not only taking Deanna but possibly little Peter Carter too.

After Carl had delivered his statement he expressed his concern for the care and safety of his son. Blake promised him that he would make sure that Jeremy was taken care of even if he had to take him in himself until Social Services could provide a home for Jeremy while Carl served his time. Blake called Social Services about the boy and they were going to send someone over right away to pick him up.

Blake could see that Carl was not a bad man but had gotten lost in his way and just needed help with his son. What he had done was wrong and he would have to pay for what he had done to two families who had thought their children were gone forever.

In the meantime Mr. & Mrs. Carter had stopped by with Peter after Blake had called them. He wanted to verify that Carl Hemp was the same man who had kidnapped Peter too. Just seeing the frightened look on Peter's face told Blake all he needed to know. Peter hid his face in his mother's arms as he cried, "Don't let him take me, Mommy!"

"Oh, I am so sorry, little boy. I didn't mean to harm you in any way. I just didn't know what to do about my son. Jeremy liked you, you know. He missed you after you ran away." Carl had tears in his eyes as he looked at Peter and tried to apologize.

The Carters were not too happy as they stared at Carl and just shook their heads and responded vehemently, "Mr. Hemp you took our child away from us. We were devastated and thought he was gone forever. How could you do that?"

Blake stepped in between the Carters and Carl before there was any physical confrontations. Carl hung his head and whispered in a choked voice, "I am so sorry! Please forgive me! I made a terrible mistake, well two terrible mistakes."

"Okay, Carl. It's time to go." Blake steered Carl away from the Carters but Carl wouldn't budge. He put his arms around his son one more time and held onto him tightly as he cried once Blake took off his cuffs.

Jeremy smiled at his father and patted his back, "Don't cry Daddy. I am okay. I am going to stay with Ashley for a little while until you can come get me."

The Social Worker, Mrs. Steele, arrived and reported to Chief Sangeovese for more information on the child in question. Both the Chief and the Social Worker came over to Jeremy to talk to him and explain what going to happen next.

As the Social Worker bent down to tell Jeremy that he was going to a nice home until his father could come and get him. Jeremy started crying and begging his father to take him home.

Carl looked helplessly at his son. "I can't take you home Jeremy. You have to go with this nice lady and stay with another family until I can come and get you. I have to go away for a while." Carl turned away with tears in his eyes.

Jeremy kept crying and looked at Deanna and begged, "Ashley, I want to go home with you. Don't leave me Ashley. Please take me home with you." Deanna whispered to her mother and pleaded, "Mommy, can't we take Jeremy home with us until his daddy can come get him? Jeremy is like a brother to me, Mommy! We can't leave him alone now." Deanna wiped away tears as she looked sadly at Jeremy.

"Blake, I can take Jeremy until his father gets out of ...well, you know until he can take care of him again. It seems the children have gotten close during this trying time. It may be better for both of them if they stay together for now."

Blake looked at the Social Worker for approval of this new situation for Jeremy. "Would this be okay temporarily, Mrs. Steele?"

"I will contact my supervisor and arrange for the paperwork to be drawn up. We will also have to schedule visits with Jeremy in this home."

"Thank you, Mrs. Steele, I think you will make both children very happy." Blake shook the Social Worker's hand.

"This is an unusual situation. It's very magnanimous of you. I will need your name and address for our records?"

"Yes, or course. It's Priscilla Wilfork. Here is my address and telephone number."

"Thank you, Priscilla, for offering to do this. As long as you think you can handle three children. I appreciate you doing this and I am sure Carl will be grateful too. If you need my help in any way, you know where to find me." Blake smiled his approval.

"Yes, Blake I feel I can do this. And, you are welcome." Priscilla gave Blake her most charming smile then continued, "Jeremy and Deanna have gotten attached to each other like a brother and sister and don't want to be separated just yet." Priscilla looked over at Deanna as she hugged Jeremy and wiped his tears.

Blake locked Carl up and explained the new arrangements for Jeremy which made Carl smile for the first time. Carl choked up and responded, "Thank you, Sergeant. I appreciate what you and the kind lady have offered to do. I know Jeremy will be in good hands after seeing how much Jeremy loves Ashley, I mean, Deanna after only two weeks. She has been like a mother to him. He will be happy with her and her family."

"You are one very lucky guy that Mrs. Wilfork is so forgiving. I don't know if I would be if you took my child. Ashley, why does he call Deanna Ashley?"

"I gave Jeremy a different name. I thought it would be a good idea not to know her real name. I know I was wrong, Sergeant. I am thankful that she is such a kind person. I didn't realize that Deanna was my boss' daughter. I would never had taken her. But…I know I shouldn't have taken any child. I have to live with the fact that I did an unconscionable thing."

"Well, you have to atone for what you did, Carl. It was unforgiveable. You put two families through torture when they thought they had lost their children." Blake nodded to Carl and left him to think over his questionable behavior.

As Blake passed by Gus he shook him awake and offered to take him home before he took Priscilla, Deanna, and Jeremy home.

"Huh, what?" Gus grunted as he tried to wake up. "What's up, Blake?"

"Hey, it's time for you to go home, old man! You have been up all night and need to get some sleep. You won't be any good to anyone like this." Blake patted Gus on the back and pushed him up from his chair.

"Okay, partner, I'm going. I can drive myself home. No problem there. You take care of Priscilla and the kids and don't worry about me." Gus smiled and waved at the kids as he went out to his car.

Chief Sangeovese peeked out from his office and called Blake aside. "Blake, why don't you get along too? I have enough extra officers on duty now. You look like you could use a nap yourself after your travels. I think I can hold the fort until tomorrow. See you at 7:00 am sharp, you hear? Make sure you have your written report to me by then."

"Ok Chief, will do." Blake was relieved and surprised at the same time. Chief must be getting soft in his old age. He wasn't about to argue but took Priscilla's hand and Deanna held onto Jeremy's as they walked out of the police station looking like a family.

"Blake, thank you, for all that you have done. I didn't think I could go on if… I am so happy to have Deanna back."

"Priscilla, you don't have to thank me. I didn't do anything here. It was Deanna who escaped on her own. She is one resilient little girl and a quick thinker." Blake's eyes twinkled as he smiled taking in the sheer beauty of this woman who had come into his life.

"Is it time to pick up Robbie at preschool yet?" Deanna's voice interrupted the adults who were clearly in their own world.

"I really miss him. Did he miss me too?"

Priscilla looked at her watch and realized it was almost time to pick Robbie up. The day had flown by with all the developments. She sighed, "Yes, he did, Deanna. He asked about you every day you were gone. He is going to be so happy to see you and meet Jeremy." Priscilla pulled Deanna into her arms again and kissed her all over her face as Deanna giggled.

"I missed you, Mommy! I can't wait to get home. Jeremy can sleep in Robbie's room in the other twin bed, huh?"

"Yes, he can. We have plenty of room for him. I am sure that Robbie will be happy to share all his toys with Jeremy too." Priscilla smiled at the two children as they held onto each other. Seeing Deanna like this made her proud to have such a wonderful daughter who would one day be an exceptional mother.

Blake bundled everyone into his SUV and headed to the school to pick up Robbie.

***

More developments were happening at the airport as the Feds and police were on the scene. However, there were some more surprises to come.

CHAPTER THIRTY-FOUR

Not Yet Over

Chief shuffled papers around his desk after giving orders to the two officers to close up Carl Hemp's house. Gus had mentioned the problem of Carl's broken window and that Carl had pleaded with the lieutenant to close up his house to prevent any burglaries. Chief readily agreed for he didn't need any more problems tonight.

Chief Sangeovese called a local handyman he knew to board up Carl Hemp's window. Chief radioed two of the officers he had pulled from the neighboring stations and told them to go to Carl Hemp's house. "Officer Bing, this is Chief Sangeovese. I need you to go to the address," Chief rattled off the street, "of this perp and wait until the handyman comes to board up the broken window. Look around and make sure there is nothing out of order there and report back to me."

"Yes sir, Chief, will do," Officer Bing replied and signed off.

"What do you think happened at the perp's house? Who broke the window?"

Officer Compton just shrugged his shoulders and sighed. "How would I know? The Chief didn't fill us in on what happened there. Maybe the perp tried to escape out the window."

"Now why would he go out the window if he can use the door?" Officer Bing shook his head in exasperation at his partner's lack of any enthusiasm.

"What's with you Compton? Did you get up on the wrong side of the bed?" Officer Bing guffawed.

"Hey, we are here. You wait here at the front door for the handyman while I check around the back of the house and the yard."

"Who made you my boss," Compton yelled back at his partner as he waited at Carl Hemp's front door on the steps feeling anything but patient.

***

Officers Jongas and Gregory reported back to the station after handing over the reins to the Feds. Chief motioned them toward two seats in front of his desk and said, "Okay, fill me in. What the hell happened out there? I got a call from the airport supervisor that you guys were shooting at the plane. God damn it! What were you thinking? Did you get the guys out of the plane before the Feds got there?"

"Well, we got one guy. The other guy ran out of the bottom of the plane and we didn't realize he had disappeared until the perp we arrested told us about him. I think he will be giving his buddy up to get some time off of his own sentence."

"Did the Feds go after the second man?"

"Yeah, they are looking for him but he had a head start."

"Well, I want you guys out looking for him too. I circulated a sketch of the guy to all squadrons in the area. Maybe we can find this guy before the Feds do. It would be a feather in my cap if we did. Now get going! What are you still sitting here for?" Chief screamed at the officers as they both jumped and ran out of his office.

Chief Sangeovese contacted the Director John Zimmer of the FBI. They spoke well over an hour covering everything. Chief knew it was going to be a long night for him since he had to put all findings into a comprehensive report along with reports from his officers.

Chief settled down after pouring a cup of strong coffee and nibbling on a leftover bagel from breakfast to compile his notes into some semblance of order for the Feds.

CHAPTER THIRTY-FIVE

Desperate Measures

Buzz pulled up to the school and waited on the street away from the pickup line for the children to come out. When a teacher walked toward his car he pulled away from the curb and rode around the block and parked further away. He knew when Mrs. Wilfork came to pick up her daughter and noticed last time she had a little boy with her too. Maybe he could snatch the little boy along with the girl. Two would get him more much needed funds. What Boss would do with them once he kidnapped them was not his concern. Boss would take over from there and do whatever he needed to do with them. He would just pick them up and bring them back to the warehouse at the back of the store and then call Boss.

Buzz wasn't all that connected upstairs, like soda without the fizz, and didn't give his actions much thought as he got out of his car and walked over to the school. He planned to tell the school office that he was coming to pick up Deanna and her little brother for Mrs. Wilfork. He had even written up a note and signed it Mrs. Wilfork.

As Blake got closer to the school he noticed the green Ford parked up the street. He looked at the license plate and recognized it as the same car that was reported by the school. He called the chief and reported seeing the car. The police had been canvassing the school area since the principal had called about the green Ford. Chief responded, "Keep an eye out on the car and I will send over someone to check it out."

Blake pulled into the line for pickup and watched the school doors for children coming out. Priscilla had headed into the school to get Robbie. Blake noticed a man making his way into the school who was unfamiliar with the routine as he pushed children aside to get inside. Without thinking Blake got out of the car, locked the doors after telling Deanna to stay put with Jeremy and that he would be right back.

Blake went into the school right behind the man. He spotted him leaving the empty office and heading for the preschool classrooms. Something wasn't right about this man. He was acting strangely. Blake felt for his gun to make sure it was there before following. He did not want to alert the man of his presence or frighten the children and staff if he had to make a move too quickly on the man.

Priscilla was talking to Robbie's teacher when the man entered the classroom and grabbed Robbie who was standing a few feet behind his mother. It happened so fast that Priscilla didn't even know what transpired until she turned around to find Robbie in the man's grip with a gun held to his head.

Priscilla and the teacher cried out in alarm. Priscilla reached out pleading with the man not to shoot her son. Robbie seeing his mother's reaction started to cry and wriggle under the man's arm.

"Mommy, I want to go home." Squirming and looking up at the man holding him, Robbie yelled, "Let me go to my mommy!"

"Please, please do not hurt my son!" Priscilla begged as she moved with caution toward the man.

"Don't come any closer if you want your son to live. I need to take him out of here now. If you try to stop me I will shoot you. Where is your daughter? I need her too."

Priscilla stopped in her tracks as the teacher held onto her arm trying to keep her back when Priscilla noticed Blake coming up behind the man. Priscilla tried to avert her eyes so as not to alert the man to Blake's presence. But the man picked up something in her eyes and started to turn just as Blake leaned forward and using the handle of his gun hit the man over the head. The man went down dropping his gun and releasing his grip on Robbie. Priscilla saw her chance to grab her son and pull him away from the man on the floor.

Robbie held onto his mother and began to cry when he saw his mother's tears. He asked, "Mommy, why did that man grab me?"

"I don't know, honey. I don't know him or why he did that. Don't worry you are fine and no one is going to hurt you. Mommy is here."

Robbie's teacher patted Priscilla's arm and hugged Robbie as she expressed her relief, "I am shocked over something like this happening in our school. Thank God Robbie was not harmed. I will call the police."

"No need to do that Ma'am, I am the police." Blake stepped forward and pulled out his badge for the teacher.

"Oh, thank goodness. It was fortunate that you were here, Officer." Mrs. Salvatore turned toward Priscilla, "You better take Robbie home, Mrs. Wilfork. This has been a harrowing experience for both of you. I will let Mr. Harden know about this."

"Thank you, Mrs. Salvatore. I agree. We plan to do just that. I am sure he must have heard about it already."

Priscilla looked over her son's head at Blake and mouthed, "thank you" to Blake who smiled and ruffled Robbie's head. He had pulled up the man who was still groggy and handcuffed him as he called into the station to report to Chief what happened.

"What's going on now, Blake? Did you find the driver of the car?" Chief asked as he wished he had something stronger to drink than this bitter coffee. He would certainly make up for that once he got home.

"Sorry, Chief. It has been a crazy week. I thought things were settling down. Most likely this man I have here with me is the driver." Blake explained what the problem was and continued, "I have Priscilla and the three children with me. I can't bring the perp into the station. Do you have another officer who can come and pick him up?"

"Yeah, I already called the two officers who are out at Carl's house closing it up. They will be there shortly. Then you take Priscilla and the children home and get home and get some rest. See you tomorrow seven sharp."

Principal Harden met Blake as he was leaving the school. Bad news travels fast. Children and teachers alike were watching Blake move the perp out to the parking lot near his SUV to wait for the officers to arrive. Mr. Harden met Blake and asked what had just transpired. Blake filled him in and was thanked profusely for doing his job.

The surprised children looked out from the vehicle and gawked at the man who was handcuffed and finally fully awake. He just stared back at them.

"Priscilla, please take Robbie and get into the car. I will wait here until the officers arrive." Priscilla didn't hesitate and put Robbie in the back with his sister and Jeremy. Once Robbie saw his sister he was back to his old self with no signs of any effects of the previous trauma. Deanna hugged her brother and kissed him multiple times much to his delight. He kissed her back and touched her hair saying, "I missed you Deanna. Don't go away again, okay?"

Deanna smiled tousling his hair as she retorted, "Okay, Robbie, I promise."

"Robbie looked at Jeremy and asked, "Who is this boy sitting next to Deanna?"

"Oh, this is Jeremy. Jeremy say 'hi' to my brother Robbie," Deanna answered.

"Hi Robbie. My name is Jeremy."

"Hi Jeremy." Turning back to his mother Robbie asked, "Is Jeremy coming home with us?"

"Yes, he will be staying with us for a little while. Okay, honey?"

"Okay Mommy."

"Who is that man that Sergeant Furelli is holding?" Deanna asked curiously.

"Oh somebody who is not a nice person. Don't worry about him. Sergeant Furelli will take care of him."

Robbie looked at his sister's hair and with a puzzled frown asked, "Deanna, where is your blue butterfly clip?"

Deanna's face blanched as she reached up to her ponytail and felt around finding nothing but the elastic band holding it together. She was clearly upset and turned to her mother, "Mommy, I lost my blue butterfly clip. I don't know where it is. I must have left it at Jeremy's house or at the lady's house that let us in. What am I going to do? Daddy gave it to me." Deanna sniffled as Robbie patted her on her arm trying to console her.

"Deanna please don't cry. I will buy you another butterfly clip, I promise. Daddy will understand. He won't be upset. He is watching over you and kept you safe and now we will go home and I will make you and the boys a delicious supper – your favorite

– mac and cheese and hotdogs. How does that sound?" Priscilla was trying to take Deanna's mind off of her loss. She knew how much the butterfly clip meant to her daughter. Priscilla whispered a prayer hoping that Deanna's guardian angel would hear and maybe find the clip. She knew Deanna wouldn't rest until it was found.

The exchange was made with the perp and Blake came back to the SUV and they drove away. The day had to get better after what they had all been through.

***

Blake looked over at Priscilla and noticed her face and looked back at the children. Something wasn't right. Deanna was crying and Robbie and Jeremy were patting her on her arm.

"What did I miss here? What's wrong, Deanna? Why are you crying? Robbie is okay and nothing is going to happen to any of you. I promise you, and I always keep my promises."

Priscilla shook her head and tried to tell Blake that Deanna didn't know about what had happened in the school to Robbie. She then blurted out what the problem was before Blake could add anything more about Robbie.

"I assured Deanna that I would buy her a new butterfly clip. She lost it somewhere. It's going to be all right."

"Oh, I see," Blake responded completely confused but just going along with Priscilla for the sake of peace.

They soon arrived at Priscilla's house and the children ran to their rooms to play. Blake stepped in for a moment. "Priscilla, I need to get home to check on my son. You are fine now. I will call you later, okay?" Blake smiled not only with his mouth but his whole face. He was relieved that this woman and her children were safe. They had become important to him and knew that he had found the beginning of a new life.

Priscilla suddenly stepped closer to Blake, put her arms around his neck and pulled him in for a long satisfying kiss. Both of them knew it was time to begin their relationship. They both had feelings that went deeper than friendship.

Neither one of them wanted to end the kiss but Blake pulled back first just to look at Priscilla's beautiful face and deep into her sparkling blue eyes. He leaned in for a quick soft kiss to seal their fate.

"Priscilla, I know it has been only a short time that we have come to know each other but I feel close to you and your children. I don't want to rush into things but I want to see more of you."

"Blake, I feel so lucky to have met you at a time in my life when I thought I would never experience happiness again. Then when I almost lost Deanna and then Robbie I realized that life is too short to waste any time. When you want to officially ask me out, well, then I will give you my answer." Priscilla smiled and kissed Blake one last time before escorting him to the door.

Blake couldn't believe what Priscilla had insinuated. She likes me, he thought. *I know she does. I think we are both ready to start this relationship.*

By the time Blake arrived at his house he was elated that his and Matthew's life would change. He plan to spend a lot of time with Priscilla and her children. He wondered how Matthew would take this news. Hopefully he would be as happy as I am, thought Blake.

CHAPTER THIRTY-SIX

A Heavenly Visitor

Priscilla fixed dinner for the trio as they animatedly talked non-stop before, during and after eating. Robbie and Jeremy had become best of friends and Robbie was excited to have a brother to play with and so was Jeremy. Robbie was hesitant at first to share some of his prized toys but when Jeremy pleaded with tears in his eyes Robbie consented.

Priscilla knew that Jeremy had always been alone and never had any occasion to play with other children. She knew he missed his father but was happy to have a place to stay and people who would love him and take care of him until his father could return.

Priscilla was relieved that her children were safe and sound and that Blake had come into her lonely life. She hoped Parker accepted her choice and that he would be happy too.

After bathing the children, putting them to bed, reading three stories and saying prayers Priscilla settled down to relax with a cup of coffee and maybe have a glass of wine before she went to bed. The kids fell asleep as soon as their heads hit their pillows. Jeremy was adjusting surprisingly well and snuggled up in the twin bed in Robbie's room with his stuffed zebra, Binky. Priscilla had put two beds in her son's room in hopes of having another child one day but that was not to be until now. She knew Jeremy may not be able to stay with them forever but she would provide for him and love him like her own. A social worker was coming in a few days to meet with her and evaluate Jeremy's needs. Priscilla planned to spend time with Jeremy working on his motor skills and speech in between the services he would eventually receive. Having Deanna and Robbie around would certainly help him too, Priscilla thought.

It had been a harrowing two weeks and she didn't ever want to go through something like this again. She found herself once again on her knees looking up to Heaven and praying.

"Thank You, God, for keeping my children safe and sending Parker as a guardian angel. I promise to try to be a better person and take the children to church every Sunday from now on."

Priscilla opened her eyes to see a bright light settle in front of her and reach out to her. Enveloped in the light was a blue butterfly clip. She reached out her hand and took it feeling a light touch so soft that she may have imagined it before clasping the clip tightly in her hand. She looked down at the clip and felt its warmth as though the clip had been heated by the light. Out of the light came the guardian angel with Parker's face.

She heard a voice, more like a whisper saying to her, *I love you Priscilla. Please forgive me for not coming back. Take care of our children and be happy with Blake. I will be watching over all of you.*

Priscilla blinked and looked all around her but there was nothing there and the light and angel had disappeared. She felt a warm feeling pass over her and a feather like touch to her lips. She touched her lips, smiled and responded, "Thank you, Parker. I love you too. Yes, I do forgive you. Thank you for bringing back Deanna and her blue butterfly clip. She will be happy to have it. Watch over us, Parker, if you can. Goodbye, my love."

Priscilla blew a kiss to the air hoping that Parker could see and hear her. She looked around one more time and hurried to Deanna's room to put the clip on her nightstand. It would be the first thing that Deanna would see when she woke up in the morning. She would know that her father had been there.

***

Blake surprised Matthew by coming home early. He thanked Mrs. Singer and told her he would take care of dinner for Matthew.

"Hey, big guy, what do you want for dinner?"

"I like mac and cheese and hot dogs, Daddy. Can you make that? Mrs. Singer makes super delicious mac and cheese. Can you make it like her?"

"Well, I will do my best, Matthew," Blake laughed at his son's response. He hoped he could do as good a job as Mrs. Singer.

CHAPTER THIRTY-SEVEN

Deanna's Surprise

Deanna rolled over and opened her eyes, stretching and yawning. She had had a dream about her dad and he had told her to be a good girl for Mommy and that he would be watching over her and Robbie and Jeremy. How did he know about Jeremy being with them?

As Deanna pushed the covers off and reached for her slippers and robe she saw something on her nightstand. She moved closer to get a better look and stared with her mouth open as she picked up her favorite blue butterfly clip. She held it in her hand and pressed her lips to it before looking up to the sky and thanking her dad for bringing it back. She knew he had found it for her. "Thank you, Daddy! I love you. I miss you so much. Thank you for watching over us."

Deanna put her precious blue butterfly clip in her hair and went out into the kitchen to tell her mother about her surprise.

"Mommy, look what I have. Daddy brought my blue butterfly clip back to me. He promised to give me a present and he kept his promise." Deanna beamed with pleasure as she stroked the clip lovingly.

"Yes, sweetie, I believe you are right about that. Daddy loves you and Robbie very much and will continue to watch over you. He is your guardian angel."

"I miss him, Mommy but I know that he cannot come back. But if he is up in Heaven he can see us all the time and watch over us, can't he?"

"Yes, he can I am sure, sweetheart. Now, go look in on your brother and Jeremy and see if they are awake. If they are, bring them out here for breakfast. Oh, Deanna, make sure the boys go potty first. Okay?"

"Yes, Mommy, I will." Deanna walked away floating along as if she had her own butterfly wings. She was so happy to have her favorite blue butterfly clip back.

Priscilla scrambled eggs and fried bacon while the toast was in the toaster. She wanted to surprise the kids with bacon. All kids love bacon.

As she shut off the gas and removed the last piece of bacon to a paper towel the phone rang. Priscilla picked it up and heard Blake's welcome voice on the other end. She turned off the heat under the eggs and gave Blake her attention.

"Priscilla, how are you and the kids doing? Do you want to come over here for dinner tonight? We can introduce our kids to each other and let them get used to each other. I plan on spending a lot of time with all of you." Blake waited for an answer from Priscilla.

"Oh, hi Blake. We would love to. The kids are doing great and Deanna has a surprise. She will want to tell you all about it herself tonight. I had one myself last night. I will fill you in later too. Thank you, Blake, for everything. See you tonight."

"Yeah, okay tonight. How about six, early enough for the kids. Then we can sit and talk about us."

"Okay, Blake. See you tonight. Look forward to it. Oh, I will need your address, Sergeant." Priscilla hummed happily as she searched for a paper and pen.

Blake gave her his address and hung up the phone smiling to himself as he thought about seeing Priscilla again.

Blake put the finishing touches on the dinner and set the table as Matthew sat and read his favorite book, *Louey the Lazy Elephant*.

Blake had made spaghetti and meatballs, one of Matthew's second favorite meals. Matthew gave his dad his approval of the choice of dinners and added, "Can we have chocolate sundaes with whipped cream and sprinkles for dessert?"

"I don't see why not, Matthew." Blake seconded the choice happily. He loved chocolate ice cream too.

Priscilla dressed the kids in their best for this special dinner. Jeremy and Robbie luckily were the same size even though an officer had brought over some of Jeremy's toys and clothes the night before.

The drive over to Blake's house was short. She hadn't realized how close they lived to each other. She unbelted the kids from their car seats and led them up to Blake's front door.

Blake was waiting there anxiety etched on his handsome face. He welcomed them all in and told Matthew to take the kids to his room to play until dinner was ready. He wanted a few minutes with Priscilla before having dinner. Before Priscilla could say anything Blake brought her into his arms and kissed her deeply holding onto her as if he would never let her go. Priscilla returned his kiss and added a few more of her own before coming up for air just in time as the kids came running back into the room all excited.

"Daddy, Deanna told me that her father brought back her blue butterfly clip!" Matthew happily announced.

"Is that right, Deanna? That is great news!" Blake looked surprised as he locked eyes with Priscilla and smiled.

Whispering to Blake, Priscilla told him quickly about her dream about the light and the clip. Blake just shrugged his shoulders and nodded saying, "I guess you will make me a believer of angels yet, Priscilla."

"Okay kids, everyone washed their hands? If not, get in there right now."

"Let me help you, Blake," Priscilla dished out the salad and brought over the dishes laden with spaghetti, meatball and sauce as the kids came filing back in to sit down where they were told.

Dinner was a success especially the sundaes which the children finished in quick order licking up every last drop.

"Okay, kids, now I have a surprise for all of you. Clean up your hands and faces and go sit down in the family room. I would like to talk to everyone and share my surprise. Hurry up now." Blake put all the dishes in the dishwasher with Priscilla's help and led her to the family room for the big surprise.

Priscilla watched Blake as he spoke quietly to the children. "We are going to be spending a lot more time together. Priscilla and I want to go out together and get to know each other better as you kids are doing. What do you think kids?"

The kids smiled, hurrahed and jumped up and down yelling and laughing, "We are going to be a family!"

Blake and Priscilla joined in and danced around and around as the kids laughed. "Well, we are not quite there yet but maybe one day." Blake smiled into Priscilla's blue eyes.

Watching nearby outside was a bright light that blinked and twinkled at the joyous display. Deanna felt a warmth suddenly coming from her blue butterfly clip. She ran her fingers over the clip and looked out the window and waved as she mouthed, "Bye Daddy, I love you."

CHAPTER THIRTY-EIGHT

A New Life

Byron was settled down in his seat on his way to Switzerland by way of Canada or so he thought as the plane suddenly stopped on the runway and began to turn around and head back to the gate. He sat up and looked out the window as several blinking lights could be seen waiting at the terminal. He knew that it was the end of the line for him.

The Feds had found Byron through a phone call that he had made to Priscilla which Blake had reported to them. Going over all calls to Leah Falls from California they also found several others dating back to two years ago. They also had connected to Ned and Smutty through the calls. Ned was willing to give the Feds all the information they requested when he was promised a reduced sentence of five years. Smutty had planned on taking a vacation back to his homeland of Serbia and disappearing there but the Feds caught up with him. They promised Smutty a comfortable place with three meals a day to live out his life – prison.

Once Byron was behind bars Priscilla and Blake met with her new lawyer and they proceeded to get her store reinstated in her name. She planned to buy out both of the partners as soon as she and Blake could get a loan. She did not trust keeping them on after what they had done to her behind her back.

Also, once the police knew the details of Parker's death and where his body was located Priscilla would receive Parker's life insurance that would keep her and the children comfortable. The LA police were going to dig up the bodies and send the remains back to their respective families for a proper burial.

Parker's will was located and everything was to go to Priscilla and the children. Blake planned to redo his own will soon.

***

After several months of dating and family get-togethers Blake and Priscilla had an important decision to make.

Life was looking up for him and Matthew and soon it would be complete. He hoped Loriann would be happy with his choice of a mother for Matthew.

Blake had an appointment with his jeweler to pick out a special item for a beautiful lady. Next he would look into adding another bedroom to his house so that each child would have their own room. Matthew would temporarily share his bedroom with Robbie and Jeremy once Blake set up bunk beds for the boys. Blake knew that Jeremy would only be staying temporarily with them. He wanted Deanna to have her own room right away. Just the same, three bedrooms would not be enough for a family of five.

With the children all safely ensconced at his house with Mrs. Singer as the sitter, Blake arranged for a special dinner at his favorite Italian restaurant for him and Priscilla. The lights were dimmed and an empty wine bottle rested in the middle of the table with a candle in it that was dripping with wax. He knew what he wanted to do as they sipped Chianti and held hands. He looked into Priscilla's eyes and then got down on his knee and took her hand in his as he asked, "Will you do me the honor of being my wife, Priscilla Wilfork?"

"Oh, Blake, yes, my answer is yes!!" Blake placed the nearly two carat diamond on her slim finger and kissed her.

Blake and Priscilla's wedding took place nine months later on a beautiful day in June with their three children, Jeremy, and Priscilla's brother, Merrill, and his family in attendance. Merrill beamed at his beautiful sister and promised to keep close watch over her and possibly move back to Maine to do just that. He wanted his son to grow up with his cousins and not alone like he and Priscilla had done so many years ago. Merrill and Carolyn were expecting their second child in the fall which made it even more urgent that he should make the move soon.

Parker's siblings called to wish Priscilla well and apologized for not keeping in contact with her. Evidently their mother had told them a completely different story about Parker's disappearance saying that he left because Priscilla had sent him away.

Priscilla sold her house and she and her children moved to Blake's house which was now complete with four bedrooms. Each child had his/her own room but spent most of their play time together in each other's rooms. The three boys insisted on being in one room with bunk beds and a twin bed and were inseparable. Maybe the happy couple would find some way to fill the extra bedroom eventually.

Jeremy had settled in with his new family but would soon be going to stay with his aunt, Cora, his father's sister, until his father had served five years in jail. Jeremy's aunt had been estranged from her brother but hearing about his problems she happily came forward to lend a hand. Jeremy wasn't happy at first to leave his temporary home but his aunt convinced him that she had a bedroom especially for him full of all kinds of toys and a great back yard to play in with swings. She also had two children around the same age as Jeremy to play with.

Priscilla, but not the Carters, decided to testify in favor of Carl being released earlier. The Carters were angry at Carl and could not forgive him for what he had done to them and their son, Peter. The judge was flabbergasted at the expression of concern for this man by Priscilla and commuted Carl's sentence but added ten years' probation.

Priscilla testified that Carl Hemp had actually saved her daughter by kidnapping Deanna before the man who was responsible for killing Parker had a chance to kidnap her. This dangerous man may have killed Deanna too. Priscilla was relieved that at least Carl was a good man and had not physically harmed her daughter. Deanna had emotionally recovered well and had forgiven Carl for taking her. She felt she had gained a brother, Jeremy, through this traumatic event.

In another dream the angel appeared to Priscilla to plead with her to help Carl Hemp and to forgive him. The angel suggested that Priscilla loan Carl enough money so that he could hire a nanny to take care of Jeremy. Priscilla agreed with the angel and went one step further and gave Carl a salary increase at the store so that he could get back on his feet and eventually pay her back. Carl vowed to work hard and do any overtime needed to repay her for their kindness for not only taking care of his son but also for lending him the money to help with his son's care. Carl's sister planned to move closer to her brother so she could help him out too.

***

Blake laid down beside his beautiful wife and ran his hands up and down her body. He couldn't believe his good fortune to have found this lovely woman. Their children had settled in and had become close in a short time as if they were brothers and sister from birth. Life was finally complete.

Blake slipped out of bed and went out to the family room when he thought he heard a noise. What he saw was shocking. In the middle of the room stood a man all in white with large wings and an ethereal light glowing all around him. Blake was speechless and felt frozen in place.

Before he could come to terms with what he witnessed the light talked to Blake through his mind.

"Please do not be afraid. I am not here to harm you. I am the image of what is left of Parker. I came to thank you for taking care of my family. I want you to know that I will watch over all of you as long as He allows me to. Love them and take care of them for me."

Blake couldn't think straight and just nodded and stared as the light began to dissipate then completely disappear. He finally got his legs to move and headed back to bed and laid down alongside Priscilla. She stirred and snuggled closer to Blake and fell back to sleep.

Blake pulled Priscilla into his arms and tucked her head onto his chest and felt complete. Soon he, too, was fast asleep and would think in the morning that the angel was just a dream, or was it?

ABOUT THE AUTHOR

J. E. Spina is a retired administrative secretary from a school system in Massachusetts. She has always loved writing poetry and children's stories.

This is the second novel that J.E. Spina has published. She has published seven children's stories and two middle-grade novels under Janice Spina. Janice is in the process of editing more books for publication.

Look for more Jemsbooks on her website
http://www.jemsbooks.com

Follow and connect with J.E. on:
Twitter: http://twitter.com/janice_spina
Facebook:
http://www.facebook.com/janice.spina.9

Linkedin:
http://www.linkedin.com/pub/janice-spina/59/321/a01/

Janice also has a blog
http://www.jemsbooks.wordpress.com
Here she reviews books, interviews and supports fellow authors, writes about her travels, talks about her venture in writing and publishing and offers helpful information for authors.

J.E. lives in New Hampshire with her husband, John, who is the illustrator of her children's books and designer of her book covers.

OTHER NOVEL BY J.E. SPINA

Hunting Mariah
(mystery/thriller/suspense/serial killer)

BOOKS BY JANICE SPINA

Children's Books (ages 0-8, PS-Grade 3)

Louey the Lazy Elephant
Ricky the Rambunctious Raccoon
Jerry the Crabby Crayfish
Jesse the Precocious Polar Bear
Lamby the Lonely Lamb (Silver Medal
Mom's Choice Awards)
Broose the Moose on the Loose
Sebastian Meets Marvin the Monkey

Middle-Grade/Preteen

Davey & Derek Junior Detectives, Book 1,
The Case of the Missing Cell Phone
(Pinnacle Book Achievement Award)

Davey & Derek Junior Detectives Series,
Book 2,
The Case of the Mysterious Black Cat

Davey & Derek Junior Detectives Series, Books 3 & 4 (coming in late summer and fall)